Old Blue

Old Blue

Stories From The Heart

PEGGY FRAILEY

ISBN: 1546407138
ISBN 13: 9781546407133
Library of Congress Control Number: 2017906946
CreateSpace Independent Publishing Platform
North Charleston, South Carolina

Foreword

"Old Blue" is Peggy Frailey's debut book, but certainly not her debut literary work, which you will understand as each story unfolds. She writes with some of the same endearing and quirky elements as O. Henry and Anton Chekhov, and with masterful character development as her strong suit (especially challenging in short stories). Peggy Frailey calls on her years as a therapist and her experiences as a mother for the personality twists that will stick like a sparkling nugget in your memory. I found myself closing both the book and my eyes after each story, to savor the journey she had just artfully led me through. Do not rush through these stories, Dear Reader, rather savor each. Re-read them and you will understand even more deeply. Themes include losing but winning, learning, age, and wisdom. They are each pure "Stories from the Heart". Her style is captivating as she changes tempo and introduces switchbacks. Each story unfolds before you with a singer's "perfect pitch" making the reading as pleasurable as the plot is engaging. We hope to see more from this talented author.

William Kenly, editor
Author of *"The Dogs of Cancer"*
"The Dogs of Luck"
"After The Diagnosis" & others

Acknowledgements

Anyone who writes knows the process involves revisions, starting over (and over), asking help from fellow writers and resource people, and never being sure your work is finished! The stories in this collection are no exception. Most originated at Rabbit Hill Writers Studio and have grown over time with the help and encouragement of teachers, editors, and fellow writers, to whom I am grateful.

A special thanks to the following:

Duncan Alderson, who gave us the amazing Rabbit Hill Writers Studio in Lititz, Pennsylvania. Duncan is an exceptional teacher and he brought out the best in our writing abilities. His debut novel, *Magnolia City*, a page-turner about Texas in the 1920s, painstakingly researched over a ten-year period, was chosen as a Must Read by Harper's Bazaar. We "students" at Rabbit Hill had the fun and honor of reading chapters of his book in progress. Duncan gives tours of historical sites from his novel, and is currently working on a sequel. Thanks also to the talented Rabbit Hill writers, with whom I had the pleasure of sharing the unique Rabbit Hill Writers Studio experience for many years.

William Kenly, author of the "Dogs" series of memoir-esque adventures, whose sharp eye and great insight were invaluable to me, and whose interest and excitement over my stories kept me motivated. He guided me through the publishing process and he and his wife, Galina, were always only an email away with help and encouragement. He is author of *The Dogs of Divorce*, *The Dogs of Luck* and *The Dogs of Cancer*, the latter book, about medullary thyroid cancer. He also published *After the Diagnosis, Medullary Thyroid Cancer Memoirs*, stories by sixty-six "meddies," which raised over $20,000 for MTC research, and placed high on the bestseller list of medical books.

Ann Stewart, writer, editor, and creative writing teacher, who taught me so much through her skillful and insightful editing. She made my stories better. Thank you, Ann! Ann is author of the heart-warming novel, *Twice A Child*, which chronicles her father's battle with Lewy Body Dementia. She also has stories in three anthologies, *Strange Magic*, *A Community of Writers*, and *Bittersweet*. Her literary accomplishments over the years are numerous, including developing the creative writing curriculum for the Capital Area School for the Arts in Harrisburg, PA, and also creating the writers' workshop for The Fredricksen Library in Camp Hill, PA.

Cindy Zollman, photographer, therapist, and long-time friend, for the cover photo, which is the way I envisioned Old Blue in the story of that title. Thank you for this image, Cindy! The photograph was taken by Cindy in Serengeti National Park in Tanzania while she was on a safari. For interested photo buffs, she shot this using a Canon 40D with a Canon 100-400 lens. To view more fabulous nature images her website is www.czollmanphoto.com.

Thanks to my friends in our writing group, including Pam Lazos, author of *"Six Sisters"* and *"Oil and Water"*, Bonnie Dorsey, Carolyn Shertzer, Sandy Arnold, Brenda Witmer, and Tom Herr. And to Linda Meashey, friend and psychologist, for her professional insight into hospitalized teenage girls regarding the story *"Breakthrough"*.

I am always inspired by the creativity and enthusiasm of my kids – Susie Hazipetros, Diane Petra, Eileen Eder, Julie Frailey, Gere Frailey Jr., Lisa Batchelor Frailey, Tom Frailey and Maggie Lee Frailey. My thanks to you and to all my much loved family and friends who believed in me and in these stories, encouraged me to publish, and promised to "buy the book."

And a special thanks to my husband Gere, my biggest fan, who encourages me in all my creative endeavors.

I hope you enjoy these stories. All the proceeds from the book will go to Doctors Without Borders, which does so much good throughout the world.

Contents

OLD BLUE

The quarrel with his daughter the night before sent Trevor out in his boat this morning, escaping the house at daybreak while his daughter and grandson still slept. He needed to be out on the water this day more than any other. He had poled the small boat away from the dock before he eventually started the motor and let the current help carry him down river to where Old Blue would be wading, fishing for breakfast.

Mist blanketed the water and partly obscured the shoreline that ran close to the channel. The hum of the boat motor was the only sound except for occasional squawks of gulls.

"You are so hard-headed," Carolyn had said last night, clanging their supper dishes together as she washed and stacked them on the edge of the sink. "You can't shut yourself up here forever. You need someone to help you."

"I can take care of myself," he'd said. Their usual stalemate. He was seventy-one and he had Parkinson's, diagnosed a few years before cancer killed his wife. He had always thought he would die first. In the long run, he'd been able to manage the Parkinson's but there had been no winning over the ravage cancer waged on Ruth's body. Soon after she died their daughter began making inquiries into retirement facilities for him, deciding he shouldn't live in this place alone.

He had no intentions of leaving his home. Carolyn could make all the inquiries she wanted, but he would decide how and where he wanted to live, something he had made clear to her numerous times. He and Ruth had raised Carolyn and Robbie here, or as much of Robbie as they had been granted, only fourteen short years, and Trevor vowed he would die here when his time came. He never said it out loud but he always believed Robbie's spirit was here, anchoring him to this place of water and mists and marshy woods.

Trevor had spent his entire life near the Bay. He knew all the small creeks and estuaries, the rivers that flowed into the northern Chesapeake---the Elk, the Sassafras, the mighty Susquehanna. The herons and ospreys and eagles that dwelled along the shores were his friends, maybe his only friends now. He sat in his boat for hours at a time studying these magnificent creatures: an osprey carrying a fish in its talons to chicks nested on top of a channel marker; an eagle with an enormous wing span circling high in the sky, scanning the water below. He especially loved watching the herons, treading along the shoreline, intent on their prey, at the same time fully aware of his nearby presence, he was sure, thanks to their full-circle vision. Those fierce yellow eyes set far back on their head could spot any danger behind or to the side. If he arrived at dawn or twilight he caught glimpses of deer foraging through the underbrush. Sometimes a raccoon. He knew they wouldn't drink when the river turned brackish, but they came to the water's edge anyway, as though trying to decide whether to take the risk.

Risk. A devil's word. He no longer took risks.

Old Blue was moving along the shoreline, high-stepping through the shallows in its peculiar ballet, knees bent backwards, like a camel making its way through desert sand. His black-capped head, with the pair of slender black plumage trailing behind, the long neck poised in a feathered S, the glaring golden eyes, all made the bird look stately and formidable.

Trevor nudged the skiff closer. As he did, the bird uncoiled its neck and in a flash stabbed the water with its powerful spear-like bill. When it threw back its head a stunned perch wiggled in its beak. The bird turned sideways then and its enormous wings began to lift as it prepared to take off to higher ground to protect its catch. Legs pushing hard, it propelled itself up and forward, wings beating, the long legs pulling up and then thrusting straight back, neck and head folded into the body until the bird became a straight line of now-graceful flight.

"Good job, old man," Trevor said quietly as he watched the heron fly away, knowing it would return for more fish.

He'd named the heron Old Blue a long time ago. He and the bird enjoyed a private society, both of them loners, both of them old. He could pick Blue out from other herons along the shore by the errant black feathers on the long gray neck. He figured nature had filled in the extra feathers to cover a scar, maybe from combat over territory. Or maybe over a good looking female heron.

Old Blue returned eventually and landed in shallow water not more than fifteen feet away from Trevor's boat, motionless, a narrow stick that stood nearly four feet tall, the general of this stretch of beach. He had stalked this particular shoreline every spring and summer for years and only a stranger would dare to encroach. Trevor had watched Blue chase intruding herons away countless times, flapping his big wings at them and emitting primeval warning croaks, long blue feathers fluttering the length of his body. An old warrior. Trevor sat very still. He knew the bird saw him although he gave no indication of it, not even a ruffling of the big wings. Trevor was accepted here, a familiar figure.

He often told Blue his private thoughts, how he'd felt when Ruth died, sometimes about Robbie. Things he had never told any person. He raised his face into the morning mist and thought about Carolyn's boy, William Trevor Perkins, carrying Trevor's name but unlike him, and unlike Robbie. Will had no mischief in his soul, not like Robbie had. A serious little kid who never said much, just watched and took it all in through those big gray eyes that were so like his grandmother's. He always saw Ruth in those eyes. Ten years old, almost a stranger to Trevor. He had never tried to know his grandson.

Squawks broke his reverie and, startled, he looked toward shore where a cluster of dirty gulls fought over a dead fish that had washed up onto the beach. The sun had broken through the mist and it would soon be hot. Sighing, Trevor backed out of the shallow water, pushed the throttle into forward and headed toward home.

They were waiting on the dock in front of the house, Carolyn with her hands planted on slender jean-clad hips, her lips tightened into a straight line, and Will beside her, all skinny arms and legs.

"Where were you! We've been worried!" Carolyn raised her voice to be heard over the motor that Trevor let idle awhile. She looked exotic, Trevor thought as he glanced up at her, with dark eyes like his and straight black hair that she wore cut short around her face. She had inherited his high cheekbones and straight patrician nose, whereas Robbie had looked more like Ruth, blond and gray-eyed. A little like Will.

Lately he thought Carolyn looked older than her thirty-four years, her face too strained, lines creasing her brow and the corners of her mouth. Worrying about him, no doubt, he thought. Or about that husband of hers, too busy with his land deals to pay much attention to Carolyn and the boy, as far as he could tell.

"You shouldn't be out there by yourself," she went on when he didn't answer her right away. "What if something happened to…"

"It's all right, Carolyn." Trevor threw her a line and shut off the motor, climbed out of the boat while Carolyn tied the line around a cleat on the dock. He followed them into the house, where he sat down heavily in a kitchen chair and allowed his daughter to pour a mug of hot coffee for him. Will had disappeared into the bedroom that used to be Rob's and Trevor could hear drawers being banged shut.

"What's he doing in there?" The noise irritated him. *Everything* was irritating him today. He propped his elbows firmly on the table to hold his arms still.

"I don't know. He's upset. We both are." Carolyn replaced the coffee pot with extra force.

Trevor braced himself for what was coming.

"You can't just go off like that and not tell anyone," Carolyn said. "And look, you didn't take your pills."

"Leave them lay. I'm not ready to take them," he said.

"Dad, I don't know what to do with you any more."

Trevor knew without looking that Carolyn was getting ready to cry. "I'm fine," he said. "You don't need to look after me."

"I promised Mother…" she stopped in mid-sentence, her face reddening.

"What did you promise your mother?"

"...take care of you." She sniffled like a child and wiped at her eyes with the back of her hand.

"I see." Trevor felt disappointed. Annoyed as he was by Carolyn's hovering, it reassured him, gave him a sense that he was still loved by someone. But a duty?

"I would have anyway," Carolyn said quickly. "It's just that... you never seem to want us around. You never did want me."

"My God, girl, what are you talking about?"

"You never even knew I was alive." She looked down at her hands, clenched together on the tabletop. "All you ever thought about was Robbie."

"You don't know...is that what this is about? Robbie?" He saw the pain in her eyes.

"Some of it. I wanted you to pay attention to me, too. It's like you went away after Robbie...well, that's all Will wants, too. He wants you to notice him sometimes. You never even *look* at him, Dad."

Trevor covered his face with his hands. Why was all this coming on him now, today? Today of all days. This girl had no idea... he couldn't begin to tell her...

"You and your mother were always so close. I would have been in the way," he said.

"You were *never* there, even before Robbie. And afterward... you hardly even came home after that." Her shoulders drooped, and Trevor thought she seemed to grow smaller in the straight-backed kitchen chair.

It was true what she'd said, he knew it. There was no way he could make her understand what it had been like for him. The awful aloneness. The rage. He had not been able to bear looking at little Carolyn. He should have taken comfort in her, a normal father would have done that, but he couldn't. God help him, he'd resented her. She reminded him too much that he'd lost his son.

Ruth had known how he felt and she'd tried to make up for his withdrawal. She had pulled Carolyn so close there didn't seem to be any room for Trevor. It was a miracle the family had survived those years.

"I'm sorry, Carolyn," he said abruptly. "For a lot of things." He stood up, feeling dizzy and as though his head would explode if he didn't get out of the house and away from his daughter's accusing eyes.

"Dad, don't leave," Carolyn protested. "Talk to me!"

"I need to go out awhile," he said.

"If you go now, I won't be here when you come back. Will and I will be gone."

He didn't know what to say to her. He was sure she wouldn't leave. They'd fought before and she'd always stayed. She'd always been there when he stormed out of the house and disappeared down river for a while, coming back after he had calmed himself.

He climbed down into his boat and started the motor, still dizzy, his head pounding now. The water frothed behind him as he moved swiftly out onto the river for the second time that morning. He grasped the wheel firmly, his vision dimmed by the spray that flew up over the bow. The speed and the salty water on his face played tricks on him. He imagined Robbie's voice, imagined him sitting next to him at the wheel.

Robbie, just turned 14, excited and twisting around on the seat of the Ruth Ann, to scan the water for surface swirls or flocks of gulls that would signal fish below. They both love the Ruth Ann, their 23-footer with the small cabin, perfect for going out onto the Bay when the blues are running, or for drifting around on the river after perch and catties.

"Let's try here!" Robbie can't wait to get his line in the water. The fishing is fast and furious for an hour or so. When it slacks off, they move farther down the river to a new spot, closer to where the river runs into the Bay. They hadn't come this far before but the swifter current might be better fishing, Trevor thinks. They throw in their lines again catching a few small blues but not enough to hold Robbie's interest. The boy is hot and restless now.

"Let's go back," he says.

"Not yet. A little longer." Robbie is disturbing the peacefulness of their day.

"Come on, Dad. It's too hot out here." Robbie climbs over the back of the seat and roots in the ice chest for a soda.

"Stop rocking the boat. Sit down."

Rob asks if he can take a swim and Trevor keeps on casting and reeling in his line over the stern of the boat, his eyes fastened on the sparkling silver lure as it breaks through the water.

Twenty-five years ago today. Like yesterday. He willed himself to stop thinking about that day. The skiff rounded the bend in the river and he saw Old Blue fishing in the shallows along the beach, his stilt legs with their backward knees dipping in and out of the water. The bird had a shadow with him, a small younger heron, its head still white and scruffy. The young bird stalked and imitated Old Blue like a winged mime.

"You old fool," Trevor murmured. "Darned if you haven't got yourself a son."

Unusual, he thought. Herons don't fish in pairs like this, and Blue sure as hell chases off all trespassers. Could this actually be Blue's son? Unlikely. The parents kicked their offspring out of the family nest as soon as they grew too big to fit inside it, he knew. They had to find their own food, get their own territory, make their own way in the heron world. Gives a whole new meaning to empty nest, Trevor thought, amused by his own humor, remembering how he and Robbie used to make up jokes for each other, corny stuff, plays on words.

Blue and the young bird made such an unusual family scene; he wished he had someone to share it with, someone who would get a kick out of it like he did. It's something he would have shown Robbie, and they would have mulled it over and over, made up stories about Blue and his family, given the young bird a name.

Maybe bring Will here? And Carolyn? He considered it for a moment, then dismissed it. Will probably was scared of the water. Trevor had never bothered to find out. The boy seemed scared of everything else around here, including Trevor. If he brought Will out on the river with him even one time there would be no turning back, he knew, not for him anyway. It could open floodgates inside him.

A shadow played across the water and Trevor looked up, awestruck as always, as he watched a young eagle soar overhead, gliding on an air current, its enormous outstretched wings in seemingly effortless motion. The bird dipped onto the surface of the water suddenly, not a hundred feet from Trevor, and then lifted itself upward, its talons empty this time as it continued its lofty surveillance over the water.

Trevor turned back to the heron, but that bird too was making its way down the shoreline. He should get back to the house, make peace, he decided. He felt calmer now. Maybe he and Carolyn could talk like two rational people. Reluctantly, he nodded goodbye to the departing herons, father and son, and steered the skiff upriver toward the house.

Carolyn's car was gone when he reached the dock. She had not left a note for him, no "goodbye, see you next weekend" or "I'll call." He was tired and restless for the remainder of the day. He hadn't expected to feel so disrupted by her departure. That night he fell asleep in his chair and dreamed fitfully about large birds that turned into wolves.

It rained the next morning and with no sunlight to waken him, Trevor slept later than usual, still in the chair. He woke up dizzy. He washed down a handful of pills at the sink and lifted the kitchen window, breathing in the cool damp air. A family of mallard ducks waddled across the yard, all in line like targets in a shooting gallery. Trevor stared, trying to blot out his thoughts. The mother, who may or may not have given birth to all these ducklings, who may have adopted a few from a less fortunate female, led the way, her mottled drab brown feathers accented by the iridescent blue tips on her strong wings. Trevor concentrated on these details. She emitted a litany of quacks to keep her ducklings in line, while the little ones, still downy brown, scurried behind her making their own chorus of soft baby quacks.

Trevor watched them progress across the yard toward the small inlet beside his house, where they slid effortlessly into the water. Family scenes everywhere he looked. He and Robbie had batted balls around on this same lawn. He couldn't shake his melancholy mood. Before he could stop them, his thoughts turned back to that day when his world had collapsed.

At first, when Robbie dives off the boat, Trevor has more of an impression than a conscious thought that his son has not resurfaced. When he realizes, he drops his fishing rod onto the deck and leans over the side of the boat looking for telltale air bubbles, or the top of Robbie's head about to splash to the surface. He sees only gray-green water.

He looks hard toward shore then, thinking Robbie might have started to swim to land. It's August, calm and overcast, the clouds and blue-gray sky reflect in the river water. A light mist bedevils the shallows and scrub along the shore. He sees no sign of anyone swimming. Robbie must be playing a trick on him. He is hiding in air pockets under the boat ready to spring up and yell "Gotcha!" He's done that before. Trevor lies across the gunwale as far as he can, sticks his head down into the water and opens his eyes, seeing only the painted red bottom of the boat.

"Rob!" he calls sharply and then screams the boy's name. He dives in and swims down as deep as he can. The current tugs at his body and drags on his legs so that he has to fight hard against it. He tries to see through the green murk but his vision is distorted. He kicks back up to the surface when his lungs start to burn. The current has carried him away from the boat and he feels the pull of it wrapping around him like a shroud that threatens to drag him back down. He struggles toward the boat and reaches it gasping, his arms like dead weights. Robbie is somewhere in this water, helpless.

Trevor continued to stare out the kitchen window at the rain, aware of the tears on his cheeks. He was frightened by how alone he felt this morning. His aloneness had been his safety for so long. There was no risk in being alone. But the comfort of it seemed gone now. He could imagine Ruth giving him holy hell for the way he had shut out the world. And Robbie wouldn't have had any more patience with him than Ruth. Rob had loved life. He had sucked the juices out of everything he did. He'd loved the river and the Chesapeake in the same way that Trevor had, with passion and acceptance of all its moods. Even its darkest moods.

Trevor hadn't allowed himself to think these thoughts before and now they flooded him.

"Robbie…" he murmured, feeling the downward spiral of his own dark mood beginning again and unable to stop the memory.

He swims all around the boat, diving and circling through the current until he is exhausted, finally grabbing onto the gunwale, panting and desperate. He spots a small cruiser moving upriver toward him. He waves frantically with his free arm. "Help! My son! Get help!"

He sees that the man on the boat is talking into a two-way radio. Help will come now and they will get Robbie up out of the water. Then they can get back into the boat and go home and Ruth will get them into dry clothes and heat up soup to warm them. Everything will be all right then.

Small crafts appear as though from nowhere. Still hanging in the water, clutching the side of the Ruth Ann, he sees the familiar shape of the marine police rescue boat approaching, POLICE emblazoned across the front of its narrow bridge. He sees two divers on the stern, air tanks strapped to their backs, face masks in place, ready to go into the water.

The divers work until dark and then the search is called off. A lot of old tree trunks, limbs, debris down there, they tell him. Wicked current. Impossible to see anything more tonight. They'll try again at daybreak. Does he need help getting the boat back? Trevor should go home, they tell him, get warmed up, call this number to file a report, and on and on. He stops listening.

After the divers leave, Trevor sits on the edge of his boat, alone in the dark, staring into the water that looks black now, calling Robbie's name. The inside of his head feels black as the water. He would like to be dead. He slides down onto the floor of the boat where he sits slumped for a long time. He picks up his son's fishing rod that the boy had left lay, runs his fingers aimlessly back and forth along its smooth surface, presses it to his cheek. The rod is bent, he'd meant to get Rob a new one. He doesn't know what else to do so he starts up the boat and returns to the house to tell Ruth. He sees the blame behind the horror in her eyes. Her screams and sobs go on all night until she finally collapses on the couch. Little Carolyn stands in the doorway and watches. They hardly notice her.

He had never told Ruth all that had happened. He never told her exactly where it happened, far downriver where the current was strong and unpredictable and where they had never swum before. He never told her, and barely admitted to himself, that in the moments before Robbie went into the water he had been glad to get the boy off the boat, wishing he hadn't even brought him along. They had been having a great day until Robbie began to spoil it with his impatience.

"Let's swim," Robbie says from the front of the boat where he is climbing around on the deck, no longer interested in fishing.

Trevor ignores him.

"Dad, I'm going in the water."

"Damn it, Robbie, just settle down, will you!"

"I'm too hot. If you won't go back, I'm going to take a swim."

"Go ahead then," Trevor says. "Take a swim and quit nagging me. Give me some peace and quiet, for God's sake." The last words he ever speaks to his son.

They had found Robbie the next day. The body…he could barely think of it as Robbie…had washed up on shore about a mile downriver from where he had gone in. People told Trevor and Ruth they would feel relieved once the body was found. Closure, they called it. But there had been no relief. Just unrelenting pain like he had never known existed.

He continued to stare out the window at the rain. The ducks had disappeared, gone off to some nearby feeding spot. The wind had come up and he could see the chop on the river. His boat bounced against the dock. He wondered if Carolyn was home, or if maybe she had taken Will with her to the shopping center, or the library, places they often frequented. He missed her.

Even as he picked up the phone he wondered if he would regret calling. He didn't know what he would say to her. He didn't know what he *wanted*. When she answered, her voice sounded like Ruth's.

"I guess I shouldn't have gone off like that," Trevor said, gruffer than he'd intended.

"Carolyn?" he said, when there was no reply.

"I'm here. What is it?"

He tried to soften his tone. "Next weekend…how about you and Will come on back out?"

Again, only silence on the other end, until finally she said, "Why?"

This was too hard. How could he explain what he'd felt like this morning, how alone he'd felt after she left? He thought about Old Blue allowing the scruffy young heron into his territory. Betraying him in a way, cracking open their private society. The bird had family now.

He squeezed the phone tightly to stop the trembling in his hand. "I want to show you and Will something."

"What?" Carolyn sounded as cold as a stranger.

"Well, if I told you now it would spoil it, girl. It's just something I want you to see because…" He began to wish he hadn't called. He should have known she'd give him an argument.

"I don't know, Dad. After yesterday…I'm just fed up getting hurt."

He closed his eyes and tried to think of the right words.

"I was wrong," he barely managed to get out. "I want you and Will here." He hesitated, the words so hard to say after all this time. "I need you two."

After what seemed like a long time, Carolyn answered with a gentler voice. "I've been waiting a long time to hear that."

Goddam, this girl was just like her mother!

"So, you've heard it now. Will you come?"

She made him wait for an answer.

"Yeah. Okay," she finally said.

He hadn't realized he'd been holding his breath until it burst out.

"But you'll have to behave. Like stay on schedule with your medicine? And not go off without telling me..."

Oh God, he thought after they hung up, what have I done? Some more royal battles ahead, he could see that.

He moved to the window and stood looking out over the water, where the breeze continued to stir up white caps. He thought how Carolyn had reminded him of Ruth on the phone, and he smiled. Slowly, he made his way into the garage and unlocked an old wooden toy box that he hadn't opened for nearly twenty-five years, not since the day after the funeral. He lifted the lid, touched the baseball bat, the leather glove, the two worn sneakers, the old mildewed life jacket, kid-sized. He pulled out a Shakespeare fishing rod that was slightly bent, a sinker and rusty hook still attached to the end of the line. He held it for a moment and then laid it gently on the floor beside him. He would put this away in his closet for the time being, where he could pick it up and hold it now and then. Will could go through the rest of the stuff in the box and pick out what he wanted. Maybe they could hit a few balls around the yard. He could probably still pitch for the boy. He squeezed his eyes shut against tears as he remembered. He lifted the old life jacket and turned it over in his hands, buried his face in it for a moment, took a deep breath. The jacket was too old and worn, no longer safe. He'd slip into town this afternoon and pick up a new one for Will.

Tossed Out

$\mathcal{M}$aura's troubles circled the garbage disposal along with the last of the macaroni and cheese, close on the heels of last night's leftover beef roast. The nearly empty shelves of the refrigerator smiled back at her. She could relax. Donald would be upset, she knew, but tonight she'd make a really good meatloaf. She'd start on it as soon as she got home from work.

Her good feeling lasted all day while she answered phones and filed reports at the insurance office. After the agents had departed at five o'clock, and the phones had finally stopped ringing, she gathered up and shredded crumpled balls of cast-off notes and spreadsheets the agents had left scattered around. She picked up stray paperclips and attached them to a small magnet, replacing them in a box in the supply closet. And finally, the last task, she disposed of half-empty cups of coffee and candy wrappers left on the agents' desks.

Cleanup wasn't part of her job but restoring some order to the office helped make her otherwise monotonous job seem more worthwhile. It gave her satisfaction and a sense of purpose, bolstered her for the evening's inevitable criticism from the man who had once professed his undying love for her. For Maura, life after five o'clock became a cloudy day.

Donald was rummaging through the near-vacant refrigerator when Maura entered the kitchen with a fresh supply of groceries.

"What happened to the macaroni?"

"I guess we ate it." She was vague. She set the groceries on the kitchen counter. "Why are you looking at me like that?"

"You did it again!"

"What?"

"The fridge. The food. You dumped everything again. Even the beef roast."

She busied herself mixing the meatloaf ingredients.

During their dinner the meatloaf tasted like sawdust to her. Donald ate without comment. Neither bothered with conversation.

The evening passed like every other. Donald disappeared into his den, where he would spend the rest of the evening logged onto his computer, while Maura sorted through a basket of clean laundry in front of the television, trying to answer the Jeopardy questions. When the show was over she turned to her newest Nora Roberts novel and vicariously enjoyed the love and passion of the couples in the book. She thought longingly of the evenings she and Donald used to sit on the couch together and talk over their day, munching on chips, kissing. They had spent hours discussing names and colleges for the children they planned to have. Donald's high-spirited twelve-year old son Randy, from Donald's previous marriage, had lived with them for a year and had added spirit to the household. Donald and she had grown even closer as they envisioned little half-brothers and sisters for Randy to play with. That had been just four years ago. *How had they become strangers?*

"Why do you suppose you needed to get rid of the beef roast?" Dr. Skylar asked the next day, after Maura had moved from talking about her job frustrations to food disposal, which was the real reason she was there. Dr. Skylar faced Maura across a large desk. Her well-tailored beige suit made Maura feel ordinary in her slacks and turtleneck top. Maura would turn thirty-five this year, but she became a whimpering child in these therapy sessions that her family doctor had insisted upon.

Her shoulders tensed. "It looked… menacing in there."

"Menacing?"

"Yes. Menacing."

"In what way did it look menacing?"

Tears burned behind Maura's eyes. She hated having to elaborate on every statement she made.

"What did it make you think of?" Dr. Skylar said.

Maura shrugged.

"Donald?"

Maura gasped. "No!"

"Do you want to throw out Donald?"

"Throw out Donald?"

"Yes. Do you want to throw out Donald?"

"No!"

"Are you sure, Maura? Your depression could be masking strong anger at him."

"Of course I'm sure. I love Donald."

Dr. Skylar changed directions, which always unnerved Maura. "Why did you need to throw out the macaroni and cheese, Maura?"

"Well, it was getting old. Bacteria starts to form after a few days…."

"But hadn't you just made it the day before?"

Maura gave up. "It was me."

"You?"

"A big pan of glop."

"Is that how you think of yourself?" Dr. Skylar asked.

"If I had any backbone I wouldn't put up with it," she said.

"With what?" the doctor glanced at the clock on her desk.

"You know…"

"You tell me."

"The way he acts now. I know he doesn't love me any more." She was sobbing now. She always ended up sobbing.

"If you didn't put up with it, what would you be doing instead?"

"I…don't…know." She blew her nose hard.

Dr. Skylar reached for her appointment book. "I want you to think about what you would do instead and we'll talk about it next time."

The end of the hour always came as a surprise to Maura. It didn't seem fair. She had spent the first half of her time talking about her job and finally felt able to talk about Donald and her, and now she was being tossed out. Like the beef roast. And the macaroni and cheese.

She resolved to stop throwing out good food. It was wasteful. Sinful. So the beef roast reminded her of Donald, even though she couldn't tell Dr. Skylar that, and the macaroni and cheese was her. Now that she had excavated that from her subconscious, she could just get over it.

The oven-baked chicken legs didn't seem quite done when she cut them apart, so Maura stuck them in the microwave to brown up the red splotches next to the bones. Donald used to like her baked chicken, especially when she used his mother's recipe. Maybe he would be nicer tonight. Well, that wasn't fair. Donald *was* nice. Wasn't he? At least he used to be.

Neither of them spoke for a while. Maura bit into the once-crisp drumstick, her eyes on Donald across the table from her. The microwave had hurt it badly. It was all rubbery. She watched Donald place his chicken thigh on the edge of his plate. He tested the instant mashed potatoes and the mixed vegetables with water chestnuts, which Maura had to admit needed more butter. Or salt. Or something.

Donald's reddening face alerted her.

"A little dried out, I'm sorry," she said hastily.

She waited---sometimes Donald offered a little cooking tip. A mention of his former wife Rebecca's kitchen skills. Or his mother's. But he said nothing. Donald's chicken thigh remained on the edge of his plate, a silent witness to her ineptness.

The grinding noise of the garbage disposal comforted her. The crunch of the chicken bones and then the final slurp as the remainder of their dinner disappeared into the unseen pipes filled her with enormous relief.

When she opened the refrigerator door to return the butter dish to its little cave, the leftover ham from the previous night's dinner looked back at her through its plastic-wrap covering. Her breath quickened. She vaguely recalled an earlier resolution to stop throwing out food. She had promised their family doctor, too, the one who had sent her to Dr. Skylar after the third miscarriage. *All those babies. Depression.* She'd heard him even though he'd muttered the words to himself as he turned away from her.

That all seemed so distant right now. She grasped the ham firmly in both hands and set it on the sink, where she hacked it into chunks before sending it down the disposal.

"I need to become a better cook," she told Dr. Skylar on her next visit. "I keep disappointing Donald."

"How do you do that?" the psychologist asked.

"A lot of ways…"

"How does he let you know he's disappointed?"

"I can just tell. His face gets red. And he tells me how Rebecca did things."

"His first wife?"

"Yes. And sometimes he tells me his mother's little 'tricks of the trade.'"

"So he compares you."

Maura bit her lip. "Oh no. He just tells me a better way to do something. He's very helpful."

"But he does get his point across, that he's comparing you, doesn't he? The point that these other women do things better. You have come to believe that, Maura."

On the way home Maura realized Dr. Skylar was right about Donald. He did compare her to Rebecca and his mother. People had always compared her to someone else. There had been Ida, four years older and a star all during high school and college. No sister could measure up to Ida. And her best friend Lorraine, always managing to be an inch or two taller throughout their childhood, and a full cup-size bigger during high school. Maura's boyish, flat-chested build paled by comparison. After awhile she had just accepted that she wasn't worth anyone's attention and stepped back into invisibility.

Until Donald…he had liked her quietness, and seemed happy that she wasn't bossy like a lot of women. He'd even told her she was a relief from his mother and his ex-wife.

Donald always seemed annoyed with her now, though. Everything was changed, since she had lost the babies. Like it was her fault somehow that she hadn't managed to give birth like his mother and his ex-wife had done. A flash of anger at Donald, and his mother, and Rebecca, and Ida, and Lorraine nearly caused her to run a red light.

Dr. Skylar decided Maura would benefit from one of her therapy groups. There were three others in the group, plus Werner, their leader, who was one of Dr. Skylar's assistants. He was a tall lean man, clean-shaven, probably close to fifty, Maura decided. The people in the group all supposedly were suffering from depression, but Maura thought their depression came out in strange ways.

The most outspoken was Suzette, an environmentalist and civil rights activist, who seemed to have anger issues, the way she always lit into everyone. Maura learned that Suzette had been arrested and jailed during a protest and was brutalized by her jailers. She told the group it was the first time in her life she'd ever felt helpless.

And then Rosie, a big-boned woman who reminded Maura of pictures of Eskimo women she'd seen in TV documentaries. Rosie had some anger issues, too. In fact Maura thought she might have a homicidal streak. Her mother had abandoned Rosie when she was very young, and Rosie had been searching for her mother all her life. Torn between rage and mother-need, she eventually ended up for a while in a mental hospital. Not such an unusual development, Werner told the group.

Maura's favorite was Lamar, an African-American with a serious weight problem and a passion for gourmet cooking. He had a gentle disposition and he spoke kindly to everyone. Maura learned that Lamar's wife and children had died in an apartment building fire some years ago and his grief had left him a broken man.

"Vee are here to look invard, and to learn to trust," Werner said, after the group members had told Maura why they were there. Werner was German, Maura figured, the way he pronounced his "w's" like "v's" and vice versa. His compassionate manner was a welcome contrast to Dr. Skylar's brusque no-nonsense style. He smiled at Maura and invited her to tell the group about her problem.

"With all the starving people in the world I can't believe you're throwing beef roasts down the fucking garbage disposal!" Suzette yelled at her. Although barely five feet tall, Suzette intimidated Maura. It was like being around Donald.

"At least you didn't eat it all yourself, like I do," Lamar said, his amiable grin going south as he looked down at his enormous belly. Maura was sure the man weighed close to 300 pounds.

They sat on folding chairs in the center of a small room next to Dr. Skylar's office. It was bare, except for the walls, which were covered with framed posters that read, "I'm okay" and "Breathe!"

"You need to tell that sonofabitch to get off your back," Rosie, the possible Eskimo, said. Maura could see that the woman worked out. Her biceps bulged through the sleeves of her T-shirt. "My man tries to tell me what to do, I kick him in the balls, and while he's bent over the damage, I smack his bald head."

Maura shuddered.

"You see how ve help each other by sharing our true thoughts and feelings. Ve have an exchange of ideas!" Pride lit up Werner's face as he looked around the group. "Our Rosie and Suzette have both come a long way in learning to defend themselves," he went on. "Ve must go slowly with Maura, she is not ready yet to do the things you vomen are advising. Wiolence is not always the answer." He looked kindly at Suzette, and then Rosie. Maura felt relieved that she would not be expected to kick Donald.

"Well, I'm glad there's *something* in here," Donald said as he pulled plastic-wrapped cold meat slices out of the refrigerator. His tone matched the scowl on his face. He slapped the meat between two slices of bread and disappeared.

Maura sighed as she arranged pork chops in a skillet. Things hadn't been like this before Rebecca made Randy move back home. Rebecca said she missed him too much, even though it had been her idea in the first place that he should come live with his father. Randy had liked her cooking and she had loved feeding him. He was perpetually hungry, like any adolescent boy. The refrigerator was always stocked, the garbage disposal silent.

Donald had been happier then, too. He and Randy used to carry their dessert into the living room after dinner and devour it while they watched television, Maura happily cleaning up the kitchen. She'd hear thumps and groans and peek into the room to see them wrestling on the floor, faces red, grinning while they pummeled each other.

She smiled at the memory as she poured frozen vegetables into a pan of water for Donald's and her dinner. The vegetables made her think of the time Randy sprained his shoulder and she had iced it every few hours with a bag of frozen peas. He had cried from the pain and then thanked her and she had felt as close to him as if he were her own son. Her wistful memories erupted in a deep sigh as she resealed the bag of vegetables and placed it lovingly in the freezer, as though she were caring for a small person.

The therapy group met twice a week and Maura began to look forward to the confidences they exchanged and the encouragement she received.

Lamar brought a special recipe for her, one of his best, he said.

"You fix meatloaf like this next time, girl, and that ol' man will take some notice. You won't be throwing this one down the garbage disposal."

"I wouldn't cook him shit," Rosie said. "I'd tell him to get his head out of his ass and cook his own damn food."

Maura laughed in spite of herself. The image of Donald with his head up his rear end was pretty funny.

Suzette considered herself an expert on men as well as the environment, especially since her traumatic time in jail. "You gotta' have more balls than they've got, or you're dead meat," she said. "Stand up to him and tell him to show you some goddam respect!"

"Like you did?" Rosie sneered.

"Shut your damn mouth," Suzette snapped back.

"Ladies, ladies, this is not productive. Ve are here to help each other, not attack," Werner intervened.

Maura listened carefully as Werner taught her how to role-play with the group, pretending each one in turn was Donald.

"Stay calm," Werner instructed. "Assert yourself, but always remain calm."

"I'll be Donald," Lamar said. "Pretend we're sittin' here eatin' supper." His voice dipped an octave as he became Donald, sounding like a growl. "Somethin' flat about this meatloaf," he said.

Maura's throat seized and her breath caught. He did sound like Donald. She swallowed and tested her voice. "I'm sorry, maybe some more salt…"

"No!" Suzette yelled. "No apologies. Tell him tough shit."

Maura said the next best thing she could manage: "Oh."

"Let's do it again," Werner said, smiling with encouragement. "Vhat would you *like* to say to Donald?"

Maura looked at all the expectant faces. "I guess I'd want to tell him…that I think it tastes okay to me, he should put some more ketchup on it."

"This is a good start," Werner said. "Ve vill put vat-you-call the finishing touches on this next time."

Maura practiced in the car the whole way home and all the next day, and each day after that. "I think it tastes fine," she said out loud. "I think it's…" no, too spineless. Suzette would jump all over that. What would Rosie say to Donald? *Shove it up your ass, Butt Head*! That's what Rosie would say. She wondered what Donald would do if he heard that! She wondered if she could say it herself.

"Shove it up your ass, Butt Head." The response emerged as a whisper at the next role-playing session. She steeled herself against the group's collective groan.

"Maura has her own style," Werner said. "She is a kind woman. She must be assertive, but kind. Always kind."

"Hmpf," said Rosie.

"Sorry you don't like it. Try a little more ketchup on it," Maura said kindly.

"Try some blood on it," Rosie said. "Yours."

Werner laughed. Maura had never heard him laugh before, only a smile. But it was hard not to laugh when Rosie cut loose.

"Let's try one more time. Assertive. Strong, but kind. Loving," Werner said.

Maura straightened her back, lifted her head high and looked directly at Werner. "Here, try some more ketchup on it. It's really a very good meatloaf, Donald."

"Better than he deserves," Suzette muttered. "The wrong person's in therapy."

With each group session, Maura's voice grew stronger. She practiced role-playing scenes in her head while she cleaned up the office each afternoon. She had come to resent the ignorant attitude of these people, totally self-absorbed, leaving coffee cups and paper and candy wrappers laying around like a bunch of school kids, not giving a thought to who had to pick up after them. These tasks no longer satisfied her. Gone was that sense of purpose. Sick of it, she practiced the role-playing techniques from group therapy. And one day, garnering her courage, she astonished the agents with a brief announcement.

"I won't be picking up after you any more," she said. "And maybe you could stop being so careless with all the office supplies?" Silence followed her pronouncement, then one of the men said, "You're right," and they all turned back to their computers. Maura wasn't sure whether she had been assertive or just plain foolish, but she felt good after she'd said it.

Werner's face reflected the amazement on all the groups' faces when Maura told them of her triumph. "Our Maura has come a long way," he said.

Lamar crossed the room and held out his hand to Maura. "That's good, Girl," he said. "You talk like *that* tonight."

"I'm making chicken tonight," Maura said.

Lamar shook her hand with vigor and pressed a packet of spices into her other hand.

"Secret ingredients," he whispered.

Donald had been grouchier than usual these days, especially when she practiced the assertiveness she was learning in her therapy group.

"This is to be expected," Dr. Skylar said during one of their private therapy sessions, less frequent since she had joined the group. "Donald feels threatened by this change in you. He is reacting."

One of the hardest things for her was to stop apologizing when Donald made a disparaging remark about her cooking. She had to remind herself to just laugh at the insult. Sometimes she noticed him studying her with a puzzled expression, like he was thinking, "Who *are* you?" And she would think to herself good, let him wonder. She hoped her new assertive, loving approach would work tonight. She had practiced so hard and did not dare go back to the group without at least trying. Tonight's dinner would be the test.

She basted the marinated chicken with well-seasoned sauce she had prepared according to Lamar's instructions, and watched the oven timer tick away the minutes. When the meat thermometer hit 165 she pulled the chicken from the oven and slid it onto a serving platter, admiring the perfectly browned skin and breathing in the aroma of roasted chicken and honey and vinegar, and Lamar's secret ingredients. Filled with anticipation, she set the platter on the dining room table in front of Donald and stepped back, watching, waiting.

Donald remained silent as he contemplated the chicken, his eyes sliding along the bird's glistening contours. He raised a quick glance toward Maura. Then, with deliberation, he picked up the carving knife and fork and cut a leg and thigh off the chicken. He passed the drumstick across the table to Maura, and bit into the thigh he claimed for himself. He chewed for a moment and then laid it on the edge of his plate.

"Did you marinate this?" he said. He pushed mashed potatoes and peas around on his plate, keeping them away from the chicken thigh.

"Yes, a new recipe, do you like it?" Maura asked. She kept her voice calm and caring. It wasn't as though Donald's response was unlike other times. She mustn't let it get to her. She had to keep remembering Werner's instructions…calm, assertive.

She slid a container of lemon pepper across the table toward Donald. "Just sprinkle a little of this on. It's really a good chicken," she said, her voice dropping to a whisper by the end of the sentence.

Ignoring the lemon pepper, Donald plopped his chicken thigh back onto the serving platter. Maura stared at the beautifully browned chicken, pretty enough for a cookbook picture, just waiting to be enjoyed by a loving couple, which is what they used to be before their marriage had turned into undeclared cold war.

As she continued to stare at the chicken, a clamor started inside her head. In slow motion she stood up and leaned across the table, reaching toward the chicken, while scenes of its careful preparation streamed through her mind…mixing the marinade Lamar had given her, rubbing it all over the chicken with such care, vigilantly watching through the oven door as the skin roasted to a perfect golden brown. Images of other carefully prepared meals streamed, one after another, with Donald pushing his food away, retreating in silences that spoke volumes. The perpetual hope that this time he would approve of the meal she had cooked for him. The crush of failure when he rejected yet another attempt to please. And now this angry red face across the table.

She'd gone to these places in rapid succession and they'd left her emotionally stranded, so much so that she didn't realize her body had gone onto auto pilot as she lifted the slippery chicken high over her head, just missing the chandelier that hung above the table. She stared at Donald as though at a person she'd never seen before, and for a nanosecond Maura had a foot in a past filled with hope and dreams, and another foot in the unbearable present. She was a stranger in a far-off land until the moment she let the bird fly and then she was just furious fed-up Maura.

"Holy shit!" Donald bellowed as the chicken flew across the table and hit him in the face, pieces of the bird sliding down his chin onto his chest, bits of skin and parsley clinging to his shirt collar, a chicken wing stuck to the front of his shirt for an instant before it dropped, like the chicken carcass, onto his lap.

Maura watched, stunned, as Donald mopped furiously at the front of his shirt and threw chunks of chicken onto the table. His mouth tried to work around the scraps of greasy chicken skin that stuck to his lips, but no words came out. His jaw dropped and then clamped shut, like a caricature of a big bird, Maura thought from somewhere in the back of the chaos in her brain. She stared at Donald's face, drained white with shock at first, now turning shades of magenta.

Donald found his voice at last and let out a stream of profanity as Maura scurried around the table and retrieved the slippery chicken from his lap before it could fall to the floor. His tirade pounded against Maura's ears as she raced toward the kitchen and crammed the chicken carcass down the garbage disposal, flipping the disposal switch so that the noise drowned out her husband's raging voice.

"You are one crazy woman!" Donald yelled as he overtook her in the kitchen and pushed past her, sounding exactly like Lamar did when he played him in group therapy. Bits of chicken fell to the floor as Donald stomped across the linoleum and Maura grabbed a paper towel to clean up the mess. Her hands shook as she wiped the floor and then shoved the rest of the chicken down the disposal. When the last piece had disappeared, she hung onto the edge of the sink and shook all over, forcing air into her lungs until she breathed right again.

She could not believe what she had done. She had never defied Donald before. Now this unbelievable act of violence. She had never seen him so angry. She felt sick in her stomach and hoped she would throw up, so she could vomit out everything that was tearing her up inside.

In that moment another sensation began, much to her astonishment. A flicker of pride competed with the nausea. *She had shown what she was really feeling and she had lived through it.* Pride was an unfamiliar sensation for her, one she hardly recognized, and it overtook the urge to vomit. She let go of her grip on the edge of the sink and, not aware of what she was doing, finished loading dishes into the dishwasher, again on autopilot as she marveled at this new sensation.

Maura looked expectantly around the circle of therapy friends, for that's how she thought of them now.

"YES!" all exclaimed, like a collective "Amen!"

"Flyin' fuckin' chicken! You let him have it!" Suzette screamed. "You're a real alpha bitch now." She raised her thumb high in universal salute to her. Maura could picture her on the steps of a courthouse waving her arms in victory over some cause, and in that moment she loved Suzette.

"You stood up to the motherfucker! You didn't kick him in the balls like I'd a'done, but you can always fall back on that later if you need to," Rosie said.

Lamar lifted his hands toward heaven with an earth-shattering smile. The man had been her mainstay since the first time she had come to the group. His loss had been greater than hers and yet his smile and gentleness, in spite of his grief, had comforted her when she thought of her own lost babies.

Werner beamed. "Ve see a big success here, our Maura has stiffened her spine. You see how ve help each other."

Maura felt like her grin was splitting her face in half.

She brushed orange glaze over the salmon fillets and set them on a shelf in the refrigerator until time to grill them. She was using a recipe from Lamar, with special herbs and spices, one that had never passed through her mother-in-law's kitchen. Randy was coming to dinner again and she could tell by the lift of Donald's shoulders that he was a happier man today. She had screwed up her nerve to persuade, insist actually, that Randy's mother allow Randy to have dinner with them every Thursday night. For once in her life, she had swallowed ethics in favor of threats when she mentioned child custody arrangements, support payments, things Maura didn't fully understand when she brought them up to Rebecca, but apparently Rebecca did. She had never stood up to the woman before but this time she had turned her alpha bitch loose.

She surveyed the refrigerator shelves, stacked with potato salad, melon balls, the salmon, all the things she knew Randy liked. Her eyes fell on the remains of last night's chicken cacciatori, conspicuous on the top shelf. Yesterday Donald had commented that the cacciatori "wasn't bad," which she considered a breakthrough compliment coming from Donald. The matter of her earlier chicken flinging had only come up once when Donald said it was a good thing she was seeing a shrink. But he'd given her a friendly pat on the butt when he said it, an old intimacy that had not passed between them for a long time.

As she stood in front of the refrigerator and gazed at the cacciatore, her fingers began to tingle.

"No," she told herself.

Not only were her fingers tingling now, but the muscles in her arms had joined in. She held onto the refrigerator door and took deep breaths.

No need to do this any more. She heard the voices from her therapy group, declaring her a winner. Cured.

But she missed the feeling of relief.

You have a choice now. Dr. Skylar's voice.

Our Maura is ready to choose for herself now. Werner.

If she had a choice now, why couldn't she choose to do it if she wanted to? What good was having a choice if you weren't allowed to choose? Choice? No choice?

She thought about how she had told the agents at work to clean up after themselves. And the way she had insisted Rebecca allow Randy come to dinner every week, something she would never have dared in the past. And then the chicken…at first she felt embarrassed when she pictured herself throwing a chicken across the table, but the memory made her smile. A backbone moment, Werner had called it.

She studied the cacciatori for a minute or two, picturing it swirling down the garbage disposal. The same anticipated relief wasn't there. She had felt much more relief flinging the chicken at Donald, and standing up to Rebecca. She heard the voices from her group again: *you don't need to do this any more.* They were right. She didn't need to do this. She didn't need to throw out the cacciatori. All that anger and sadness she had been flushing down the garbage disposal had dissipated, her babies a tender memory.

She pushed the refrigerator door firmly closed.

Drumbeat, Heartbeat

*T*he drums brought John back to the pueblo. Their steady beating had conjured up images of moccasin-clad ancestors, finally breaking through his grief and leading him home to Taos Pueblo. He knew the rhythms he heard now were recordings drifting over the dusty compound of the pueblo, playing from the main building to create atmosphere for the tourists. But they kept him anchored to the earth like nothing in the East had done.

He stood behind a wood plank table in front of his pottery shop and watched the tourists amble around the dusty compound with their cameras and camcorders. He wore his habitual jeans and sleeveless denim shirt, his black hair grown longer these days, touching his shoulders and gleaming in the sunlight.

The sights that seemed to intrigue the tourists were a part of him, familiar landmarks of his years at the pueblo. Sometimes he knelt inside the old Catholic church with the cross on top, although it was harder to relate to the Catholic god of his youth since Emily. His gaze fell on the adobe mud dwellings across the creek, multi-story buildings with painted blue doors and ladders to the upper levels leaning against the walls. Some were still oc-cupied by Pueblo families despite the absence of electricity and running water. His grandfather continued to live in one even though John and his mother urged him to move to a more modern house.

Rows of shops lined the compound on both sides of the stream, and many of the artists had set up tables like John's to display pottery and turquoise jewelry, small leather drums, an occasional table of wooden toys. John's aunt baked flat bread in an outdoor oven near his shop. He could see her now as she pulled loaves out of the adobe hornos, her colorful blue and red striped dress looped over her shoulder and pinned at her side with polished silver quarters that sparkled in the sunlight. He envied the ease with which she talked and laughed with the tourists who stopped to sample her bread.

It was the kind of day that reached deep into John's soul. The late summer sky was blue and cloudless. Red Willow Creek, "The River," made its way through the center of the pueblo, flowing from the sacred Blue Lake high in the mountains above Taos, where no white man was allowed. A breeze stirred the leaves on the red willows and aspens along the stream. Mockingbirds called from the tree branches.

"This is lovely, did you make it?" A woman held one of John's bowls, turning it in her hands. Sunlight reflected the buried mica like gold in its polished red clay surface.

She was almost as tall as John and wore blue slacks and a white tee shirt with flowers clustered across the front. She might have been thirty. She reminded him a little of Emily, with the same erect posture and direct blue-eyed gaze, taking on the world.

"Yes, I did," he said. He had made it during the winter, when the temperatures had dropped so low that he hadn't the heart or stamina to roam his beloved Sangre de Christo mountains, as he had always loved to do. Instead, he had shut himself up in his shop, a radio his only company. But even before spring arrived, fighting cabin fever, he had dragged all the pots outdoors into the sunlight.

The woman replaced the pot she held and walked the length of the table, examining each piece.

"So beautiful," she said. "If only I could create something like this." She smiled at him, her eyes blue like the Taos sky.

The pots were typical of Taos Pueblo pottery, plain and made from the micaceous clay that John dug from the nearby hills. Each pot took him many hours to create, smoothing the coils of clay together with his hands until they became a seamless rounded vessel. The cool wet feel of the clay and the endless smoothing and shaping had calmed him during the past months.

He couldn't find his voice to explain this to the woman, although he would have liked to. Instead, he nodded silently.

"These are *all* beautiful, it's hard to choose." Her hands hovered over the pots as though she would like to gather them all to her. Her voice was soft, with a musical quality like Emily's. Her eyes held his with a directness that stirred him.

"Take your time looking at them. There is no hurry." He straightened his shoulders and felt a slight loosening of the tightness that was always inside him now. He remembered feeling like this the day he and Emily had first talked.

He pictured her now as she had looked that day in the chemistry lab at the university, flustered, her short brown hair rumpled on top from repeatedly running her hands through it. They were grad students starting a new semester.

"Help!" She had sat down beside him at the lab table and pushed a thick workbook toward him. "You know this stuff. I don't get it. I'm lost."

He helped her with a lab experiment and then as a thank you she cooked him dinner in her small off-campus apartment. They began to see each other. He looked forward to her light-hearted manner, the easy way she talked and drew him out of his shyness.

"Tell me some more about growing up at the pueblo." And he told her stories of his youth there.

"We'd climb up on the roof of the houses and race each other up and down the ladders. We had to jump a lot because some of the roofs were higher than the others. The old people down below would yell up through the roof at us." The memory always made him laugh.

"What'd they yell?"

"Who knows, it was all in Tiwa and hard to hear when we were on the run. Something to the effect of 'go far away, you bad coyotes.' We just kept running."

She called him a fearless warrior. She wanted him to come into her bedroom and make love to her but he said no, they must wait until they were properly married.

"My parents don't want us to get married," she said. "They say there are too many differences. Cultures, religions, you know."

"Mine say the same thing," John replied.

When Emily turned twenty-two, they married in her family's Presbyterian church in Phoenix. She had worn a long white gown and veil and John had rented a tuxedo. Emily's best friend was her maid of honor, dressed in pale green satin, and another friend served John as best man. His parents did not attend.

They had returned to Taos and married again in a traditional Pueblo ceremony in the woods, performed by a priest and followed by a feast and dancing. Emily had looked beautiful in a more simple long white dress with daisies twisted into a crown on top of her short brown hair, sun bleached now. John thought she'd looked like a wood nymph. This time *her* parents did not attend. He'd understood, but he wished that their parents could be united with the two of them on this day.

He had accepted a research job with a pharmaceutical company in Connecticut as soon as he completed his fellowship at the university. They both cried as they drove across the New Mexico border and headed east, and they felt displaced in their small city apartment in New Haven, so different from their apartment in Phoenix. Cold seeming, without the earthen colors of western homes. Emily had found a job in a book store while she waited for a teaching position to open up. John could tell by the expression on her face sometimes that she was homesick, although she did not say so.

"I'm going to quit," he said more than once. "We'll go back to Taos. Or Phoenix. I can get another job."

Her optimism and strength carried them at these times. "You're doing important work," she said over and over. "We'll get used to it here. Come on, Johnny, cheer up, take me to bed and make a baby for us."

She had been unable to get pregnant. When the doctor confirmed this, it was John's turn to be the strong one.

"I don't need kids. Just you," he told her.

He realized with a start that the woman in front of his table admiring his pottery had asked him a question.

"How much is this one?" she said, her smile and tone suggesting she had already asked the question.

He told her the price and saw her eyes widen.

"It's more than I can afford," she said. She appeared to think hard. "But I'm going to buy it anyway. I want it."

Emily would have done the same thing, he thought. Follow her heart. His hands shook while he wrapped the bowl and placed it carefully inside a packing box.

The woman wrote a check and held it out to him, her fingers brushing his hand for an instant.

Emily's hand had felt dry and hot that last afternoon, her fingers fluttering inside his steady grasp. Her parents had arrived the day before, aware they were there to say goodbye to their daughter. He had seen blame in their eyes along with grief when they had turned from Emily's bedside and looked at him. Blaming him for taking their daughter so far away from them.

He had held a glass with a straw to Emily's colorless lips and urged her to drink, but she had looked at him helplessly, too weak to swallow. He was glad her parents had left the room for a while, leaving him alone with Emily. The gray walls in the hospital room had closed in on him as he sat on the edge of her bed. He had clung to her hand and stared at the bag of liquid morphine dripping into her arm. He detested the sight of it.

"Make good life…for yourself," she had said, so low he had to bend close to her face to hear the words.

"I can't without you," he whispered.

"Yes…John…y…get married." It was hard for her to breathe when she talked. "A woman to…give you…son."

He knew their childlessness still haunted her, even as she lay dying. "You are enough for me. Always," he said.

For weeks after she had died, he sat in their darkened apartment, hearing the beat of Indian drums from somewhere deep within his consciousness. Sometimes he felt Emily's hand on his cheek. After a while her voice faded and his sobs no longer contained tears. He had returned to Taos, life flat and colorless.

"I have to carry this on the plane." The woman's words pulled him out of his reverie.

He glanced at her check. Her name was Mary. Slowly, he constructed a handle of packing tape around the box so that she could carry it more easily.

"Well, thank you," the woman said, lingering. John thought about asking her to have a cup of coffee with him, or a cold drink. He could invite her to the small restaurant at the edge of the village, where they could sit in the adobe coolness and talk.

"I'll take good care of this." She tapped the box and smiled at him, waiting. They stood looking at each other for what seemed a long time to John. His head filled with steady drumbeats. He let his gaze wander over the tops of the cottonwood trees to the cloudless sky, deep as the sacred lake high in the mountains above the pueblo. He heard the gurgle of the stream and the mockingbirds' songs from the tree branches. This is the way he had seen and heard it all when he was a boy, fresh and new.

He brought his attention back to the woman. She was turning away, holding the package he had wrapped so carefully tightly against her.

He felt Emily's hands on his back, pushing him lightly. "Fearless warrior," he heard her say, her words mixed in with the drumming inside his head. And his own words, "You are enough for me, always."

He watched the woman walk slowly toward the exit gate, past the old church, her image growing smaller and smaller under the cloudless sky. He continued to watch even after she had disappeared from view.

Down For The Count

*T*he bricks did him in again. If he hadn't stopped outside the store to count them, he'd be a free man. He had seen the old man at the cash register watching him shove a bag of noodles under his jacket, and when the guy picked up the phone, Conrad knew he was calling the cops. The old man yelled "Hey you!" as Conrad raced out the front door with his heart pumping so hard he had to stop and catch his breath. The bricks caught his eye as soon as he stopped. Neat rows of them, red with white edging, all along the curb, sprigs of grass and weeds growing up between them. Seven, eight, nine, ten…

The cruiser pulled up at the curb as Conrad got to number fifteen. Two cops, one tall, one short. They stared at Conrad staring at the bricks.

"That's him, grab him!" the old man bellowed from the door as though Conrad were in flight.

"Don't want any trouble," Conrad said, distracted but lifting his arms in surrender. When he did, the bag of noodles fell out the bottom of his jacket and onto the sidewalk. *I'm done for,* he berated himself silently. *I am such a fuck-up.*

Inside the county courthouse, the judge pronounced sentence while Conrad counted the number of pinstripes up and down his public defender's suit. Eight on each shoulder, another twelve across the back. You'd never know this guy was his poor dead ma's brother, who never even bothered to come to her funeral. He'd let Conrad know in certain terms that he only took his case because the judge ordered it.

"Mr. Shaltzhammer, are you listening?" The judge's voice pierced through his mental haze.

"Yes, Sir." Conrad tried to concentrate on the judge's face.

"I don't want to see you in here again."

"No, Sir." Conrad tried to calm himself with deep breaths. When that didn't work, he dropped his gaze to the floor and made note of the pattern in the tiles: three rows of three diamonds each in every block. He wished he had time to be more precise, but his uncle-lawyer was pulling him toward the back of the courtroom.

"Come on, move. For Christ's sake, you're in outer space."

"So what'd I get?"

"You didn't hear him? You really are on another planet. What is it with you?"

"Just tell me what it is this time, okay?"

"Okay, here's the deal. You got probation for a year and community service, six months. You won't have to go back to a cell. Unless you fuck up."

Conrad liked the cell he'd been in. Easy free food and a lot of bars to count.

"What's the community service?" he asked.

"Just the place for you. A job at St. Philomena SED Camp."

Socially and emotionally disturbed kids. Summer camp for fucked-up kids. Conrad shuddered. He'd rather stay behind bars.

"We're going there now," his uncle said. "Nice little Poconos retreat. Not Caesar's Palace, but hey, what the heck."

"My stuff?" Conrad thought of his few articles of clothing and his stash back at his place.

"We'll stop for it. You won't need much."

Conrad followed his lawyer-uncle out the door of the court-house. The blast of the hot June air brought him back to reality. In all his nineteen years, he had never felt this trapped. He could make a break for it but where the hell would he go?

"Can't live through this," he said under his breath. "I'm dead meat."

"What's that?" his uncle said.

"Nothin."

With skin as white as new snow, a definite disadvantage on the streets, and with a face that he wanted to cut sometimes because he looked like some fuckin' choir boy, Conrad nevertheless had survived the streets, juvie, even his old man. He'd learned how to take care of himself long before his ma died and before his old man got even crazier than before. He'd moved out after the funeral, found an abandoned warehouse to squat in, and got along a lot better by himself. There wasn't anyone left he cared about any more. Especially not this fancy-suited uncle who had never lifted a hand to help his ma when she got so sick, and told Conrad he'd only taken his case because Conrad's PO had called the judge. The judge and the PO had insisted Conrad's uncle take his case.

His ma hadn't been too sharp herself but she'd made him go to school. He'd managed to stay on the rolls at St. Andrew's without spending much time there. One of his teachers had been okay. Sister Kathleen. She said he had a good head for figures. She knew how to explain things to him so that he understood. She'd wanted him to finish school, but he knew he'd never make it in a straight world anyway. Not when he couldn't read the right way. He kept seeing things on the page that they said weren't there. He finally quit trying to figure it all out and did his best to get by on his wits, what there were of them.

"Conrad, you were just standing there staring at the sidewalk when they arrested you," Sister Kathleen had said one time when he'd been picked up. "Why?"

It was the bricks in the sidewalk that time, too, but he didn't answer her. He didn't want her to know he was such a stupid crook. He'd get to counting things and forget what he was doing. That's how the cops caught him so often. It always embarrassed him.

Now he sat hunched over in the front seat of the car with his uncle, knowing where he was heading would be even worse than school or jail. His uncle was cracking gum and slapping the steering wheel of the car trying to keep time with the crap coming out of the car radio. The inside of the car smelled like Juicy Fruit. If he could count something, he would feel better, but the car was moving too fast to get a bead on anything.

He had heard about St. Phil's one time from a guy in a cell next to him. It sounded like a bad scene, nuns running around messin' with everyone's head and crazy kids yellin' and trashin' the place. Man, he'd left home to get away from that shit. And now he was going to be stuck there for six months. Without parole.

"Almost there." His uncle turned onto a dirt road that wound through a small forest of pines. He stopped the car in front of a long worn-out frame building that stretched beneath tall oaks. Conrad followed him into an office crammed with unmatched file cabinets, some old metal work tables, and a First Aid station. It smelled like the infirmary at the jail, heavy on alcohol and adhesive tape.

An old woman dressed in a dark blue skirt and white blouse and some kind of white scarf on her head, a nun, Conrad figured, sat behind one of the work tables. She stood and came around the table as though she had been expecting them. She didn't even reach Conrad's shoulder, and she wore Reeboks, something he'd never seen a nun wear before. Her eyes, storm blue and fierce, were unencumbered by glasses, which surprised Conrad because the old gal was at least ninety years old if she was a day and couldn't possibly still be able to see that well. Conrad remained fixed on her eyes. They were slanted up like the cat that used to live with him and his ma. He'd loved that cat. For the first time in his criminal career, Conrad forgot to count.

"I'm Sister Bernard," the nun told them, not taking her eyes off Conrad. His lawyer might as well not have been there. "Mr. Shaltzhammer, we intend to keep you very busy," she said. "There will be no time for any criminal activity here, whatever it is that you do, and I will expect you to fulfill your obligation to us and to society while you are here."

Whatever it is that you do? She must not know shit about his record. The B&Es, the scams when he could remember to do it right, the store stuff. He never touched cars, except an occasional hubcap, and he never hurt anybody. It was a point of honor with him. He wasn't the best at his trade, but he usually got by, when he didn't get caught. If this nun didn't know all about it, well maybe he could work it some way.

"As you probably were told, we have very special children here," Sister Bernard said. Conrad watched her mouth forming the words and longed to count something on her. Her skin was smooth for such an old broad, so no wrinkles to work on. No pleats on her blouse, nothing to count on the skirt. No stripes, no dots. Sweat beaded on his forehead and his armpits felt wet. He searched the room for some columns, a railing.

"Mr. Shaltzhammer." Sister Bernard's voice startled him. "I expect you to look at me when I speak to you."

"Yeah, sorry," Conrad said.

"The correct reply is 'Yes, Sister.'" She stared directly into his face, still ignoring his uncle, who was concentrating on his wrist watch when Conrad glanced toward him for some backup. "Now, I will expect you to be helpful to the children, along with your other duties. And remember, you will be an example to them. No swearing, no cigarettes, no drinking while you are here. No drugs, brought in or sold. No stealing. Do we understand each other?"

He'd never make it here, wouldn't last a day. He'd make a break and it'd be back to jail and that would be a relief. He spotted a cup filled with pencils on the table and counted frantically… two, three, four….

"You'll start off in the kitchen and do whatever Cook needs," Sister Bernard said. Conrad mentally flashed on an army drill sergeant in an old war movie he'd seen. The nun nodded toward the door, face expressionless. "Take your bag to the dormitory next door and then go around the back way to the kitchen." She nodded curtly toward Conrad's uncle and turned back to her work table.

Conrad's uncle accompanied him to the dormitory, distaste written across his face. "Tough old broad," he said. "Good luck with that one." He pointed to an empty cot and Conrad dumped his bag on top of it.

The two stood outside a minute later, neither saying anything. Then Conrad muttered goodbye to his uncle, his last contact with the outside world, and shoulders slumped, headed toward the kitchen to begin his sentence. Looking back, he glimpsed a weak wave of his uncle's hand as the man hopped into his car and sped away, kicking up dust and gravel in his wake.

Peeling potatoes was nothing new to him. He used to do it for his ma. Not this many, of course. He never saw this many potatoes before. "That's enough now," the cook told him eventually, pointing a long-handled fork at the pyramid of potatoes on the table. Conrad had lost count at one hundred and fourteen. The cook's voice sounded hoarse, when he actually talked to Conrad. Like his old man's had sounded. Conrad glanced at the tattoos on the cook's arms, a ship's anchor on one and a big heart with the name Helen scrolled across the other one. Navy guy, probably.

The clock on the wall of the kitchen hung cockeyed and he longed to straighten it. After a while, the cook left. Conrad figured he was headed for the john, so he slipped out in the opposite direction, reaching for cigarettes he'd stuck in the waist of his pants. He found a clump of bushes that seemed hidden from view, took a leak, and lit up a cigarette. He inhaled deeply and relaxed for the first time since court.

"There is no smoking allowed here," a stern voice came to him from the other side of the bushes.

Conrad jumped. *Surveillance cameras out here?* He snubbed out the cigarette and with the toe of his sneaker pushed it into the dirt under the bushes.

"Come out here please," the voice ordered.

Conrad squared his shoulders and strolled as defiantly as he knew how from behind the bushes. Sister Bernard and a girl about Conrad's age waited. The girl wore shorts and a striped T-shirt, stark contrast to the nun's dull garb. The girl had impressive boobs, Conrad thought. A dust of light brown freckles across her nose set him counting…five, six, seven…

"As I told you before, there is no smoking allowed here. Throw your cigarettes in the trash can behind the kitchen. Your counselor has already removed the cigarettes from your bag. And your marijuana. Did you really intend to use that here?"

Conrad looked at the ground while the nun continued to stare at him. *They had gotten into his bag!*

"Do we understand each other yet?" the nun said.

Conrad nodded.

"Yes, Sister," Sister Bernard corrected him.

Conrad forced himself to comply. He decided then and there he would make a break the first chance he got.

Dinner was a hearty meal of mashed potatoes and sliced turkey, and Conrad stuffed himself until he couldn't eat another bite. He hadn't had food like this since his ma died, and not much of it before that even, after she got sick. He was expected to help clean off the tables but instead, he sat still and tried to make his plans.

"Why are you lining up all the water glasses?" The girl who had been with the nun slid onto the bench beside him.

Conrad looked at the row of squat glasses he had arranged in a parade of dwarf soldiers. "Just foolin' around."

"I'm Anne Marie." She smiled and her whole face lit up.

"Conrad," he replied.

"I do crafts with the kids." She swallowed some milk out of a half-pint carton, dripping a little of it down her chin. Conrad watched, fascinated. She was wearing the same shorts and striped T-shirt. Conrad had counted four stripes before he realized he was staring too long at Anne Marie's breasts.

"Kitchen," he said, eyes lowered. She was pretty and probably a rich girl and he definitely didn't know how to talk to her.

"That's where all the new ones get put," she said. "Cook's a good guy."

"Gotta' go," Conrad pushed himself off the bench and headed for the dormitory.

On his second day in the kitchen, the cook added carrots to Conrad's responsibilities. Conrad had been watching the cook disappear behind the trees now and then. He could smell smoke on him when he came back inside, and he could almost taste the tobacco himself. He noticed a flask in the cook's back pants pocket, too.

When at eleven o'clock the cook took off his big apron and told Conrad to keep peeling carrots, Conrad laid down his peeler and followed the man to a secluded spot behind the kitchen. The cook was in the process of uncapping his flask when Conrad sauntered through the pine needles.

"How about letting me have some of that?" He figured he'd either have a good drink or get sent back to jail, a win-win situation either way. He hoped the cook would be frightened enough of Sister Bernard to give him a drink, just to keep him quiet about the flask.

The cook merely looked disgusted. "Punk kids. Don't drink it all. That's enough." He yanked the flask back out of Conrad's hands. "Now get back in there and peel the goddam carrots."

Feeling better than he'd felt in days, Conrad resumed peeling, humming a little under his breath. His head felt clear now, clear enough to start planning his escape. He'd go back to his bunk and wait until after dark, then he'd make his way out to the highway and somehow find his way to the next town. He hadn't gotten any farther in his planning before one of the counselors stuck his head through the kitchen door and motioned for him to come outside.

"Sister Bernard wants you, man. Come on."

What now? The cook wouldn't dare rat on him or he'd get thrown out himself. He followed the kid, who wasn't much older than him, toward the long low building he'd come to dread.

"You have disappointed me," Sister Bernard said, standing as soon as he walked into the make-shift office. "I clearly told you the rules here. No smoking, no drugs, no drinking. In the short time you've been here, you've violated two of them."

Conrad examined the toes of his sneakers. The cook must have ratted on him after all.

"What do you want to tell me about this?" Sister Bernard said. "Look at me when I speak to you, Mr. Shaltzhammer."

Conrad raised his eyes and met an intense blue stare. A laser might feel like this. "I don't know," he said.

"No, I don't suppose you do," the nun said. "Well, I'm adding to your kitchen duties. You need something more to occupy your time, I can see that."

Conrad looked past her to the tin of pencils on her desk and started counting…five, six, seven…

"Tomorrow morning at six o'clock I want you to go to cabin number seven and get Sammy O'Hara, and bring him to the dining room for breakfast. Your counselor will tell you how to find cabin seven."

Conrad nodded. He didn't plan to be here at six o'clock tomorrow morning. Whoever this kid was, he'd have to find his own goddam way to breakfast.

Fresh air that he wasn't used to, and the nips from the cook's flask, plus tokes from one of his cabin mate's stashes all combined to knock him out early that night. His head had no sooner hit the pillow, or so it seemed, than a counselor was yelling at them to get their butts out of bed and over to the dining room for breakfast.

Shit. He'd missed his chance to escape, and now he had to go get some kid in cabin seven, whoever he was.

The small green frame cabins were laid out in a row behind the office building and cabin seven was easy enough to find. Conrad hurried up the porch steps and through the screen door. Everything smelled old and wet, like the cellar in his ma's house. A shriek stopped him in his tracks.

"Get your fat ass outa' here, you skinny fart!" Something big and heavy…a suitcase…came airborne in Conrad's direction and he ducked just in time. Street instincts took over and Conrad was across the room in seconds, had the boy's arms pinned to his sides. The kid was soft and fat. Conrad heard him gasp, felt him twist and spit on him.

"Lemme go, you fuckin' asshole," the boy yelled.

"Shut up," he said against the kid's head, tightening his grip around the boy's arms and chest. He jerked the boy off his feet and kneed him in the back of his legs, causing the boy to drop belly-down on the floor. Conrad was on him in an instant, straddling him and putting a hammerlock on him. The only other class he had liked at school besides math was P.E. because the wrestling coach taught it and showed them a lot of dirty tricks. He wiped the saliva off his arm onto the kid's shirt.

"Lemme go," the boy continued to yell. Conrad decided he couldn't be more than twelve or thirteen. "Get the fuck off me."

Conrad continued to hammerlock the boy until finally he grew quiet and lay still.

"Okay, get up," Conrad said then. "But keep your filthy mouth shut and no more of this crap or you're back down for the count. Got it?"

The boy nodded. He was crying.

"Oh, shit," Conrad said. He had never cried, no matter how hard the old man had beat on him.

He yanked the boy to his feet and half pushed him out the door and down the porch steps. "You give everyone this much trouble?"

The boy sniffled and waggled his head as though he didn't know the answer.

"Come on." Conrad set off at a fast pace along the dirt path that led to the dining room, the boy following. He was hungry and wanted some breakfast.

"What's your name?" he said over his shoulder.

"Sammy."

"Well, Sam-o, you better start keeping your mouth shut 'til you learn how to fight. Someone's gonna kill you one of these days if you don't." The thought appealed to him.

He led Sammy into the dining room and through the cafeteria line. It smelled like some of the better soup kitchens he'd eaten in back in Allentown. He winced from the racket as he and Sammy carried their trays of sausage and gravy-soaked biscuits to a long vinyl-covered table. They squeezed onto a bench between a row of adolescent boys shoveling in biscuits and gravy and yelling at each other through mouthfuls of slush. It seemed a lot like the jail mess to Conrad, only these inmates were smaller.

He made his break that night, after the other guys in his cabin were asleep and the campgrounds looked dark. His cabin mates were older than a lot of the brats at the camp and slept soundly, thanks to the pot they had liberated from the counselor. He shoved his extra jeans and shirt in his canvas bag, all the possessions he had brought with him. The rest of his stuff was still back at his place, where he intended to head when he got out of here.

A faint light from the nun's office lighted the path slightly, and he skirted around the building through the pine woods. If he remembered right, he was going in the direction of the road. A screech owl startled him and he froze. That's when he heard rustling off to the side. A raccoon or something, he decided when nothing appeared. He kept going, bumping into trees and once tripping and falling.

"Damn." He rubbed his knee and was getting back up when a bright light shone in his face.

"Going somewhere?" a voice said and Conrad recognized the same kid who had pulled him out of the kitchen the other day.

"Son of a bitch." He was getting sick of this stool pigeon. He held up his canvas bag. "Got a good pair of jeans in here. Forget you saw me and they're yours."

The boy laughed and gave Conrad a push toward the path. "Someone wants to see you," he said.

Sister Bernard looked pissed when the counselor led him into her office and Conrad cringed. The nun didn't even stand up, she stayed behind her table and kept tapping a pencil on the metal top. What the fuck was she going to dream up for him to do now? Hopefully send him back to jail.

"What did you think you were doing, Mr. Shaltzhammer?" Sister Bernard said, her voice quiet, controlled. It scared him. His old man used that tone before he lit into him with his fists.

Conrad thought it was obvious what he was doing, so he didn't reply.

"Look at me."

Conrad snapped at the order, the nun's fierce blue eyes pinning him again.

"You are here on probation, not at your leisure," the nun said. "In just a few days you have managed to break every rule of this camp. The judge could have sent you to jail, but he gave you an alternative, a much better alternative than jail. However, I am inclined to send you there right now."

Conrad froze. The old broad wasn't fooling. She looked even more pissed, if that was possible. Earlier he had thought jail would be better than this, but now he wasn't so sure. He thought fleetingly of Anne Marie before he noticed the pencil holder on the nun's desk and began counting feverishly...three, four, five...

"...one more chance," the nun was saying. "Possibly your last one."

Here it comes. Clean the latrines...he'd done that before... scrub out the cabins, wash dishes every night. He could handle it...eight, nine, ten pencils...

"Sammy has been a challenge to us. But he appears to admire you. I'm not sure that's such a good thing, for him to admire you."

Neither was Conrad. "He's kinda' like I used to be," he said.

Sister Bernard nodded. She didn't seem surprised. "You are to teach Sammy how to multiply."

Alarm swept through Conrad like a flash flood. "I can't..."

"Yes, you can," Sister Bernard said. "You have a good head for mathematics. I have it on good authority."

Sister Kathleen? Do they know each other?

"Come to the dining hall tomorrow morning as soon as you are finished in the kitchen. Sammy will be there. There will be paper and pencils. I want you to start with the multiplication tables."

"Not him…." he started. But Sister Bernard had turned back to the stack of papers on her desk.

He was fuckin' down for the count this time.

Conrad didn't sleep well that night. He had nightmares about large numbers tumbling over each other and fat boys chasing him. He got out of bed before the counselor came in to yell reveille and made his way to a big oak tree near the dining hall. He flopped down on the grass and desperately counted limbs on the tree. He wished his ma was alive so she could explain all this shit to him. How this nun could see into him like one of those X-ray machines. He didn't notice Anne Marie until she crouched down next to him on the grass.

"How's it going with Sammy?" she asked.

Conrad tried to resist counting the stripes on her T-shirt and got up to three before he stopped himself. "I'm supposed to teach him numbers." He wasn't too worried about that part of it because Sammy's head worked a lot like his own. And Conrad knew the way to teach this shit to him, the way to get him to pay attention and remember, like Sister Kathleen had done with him. What really worried him was having to spend more time with Sammy. The kid bugged him.

"You'll be a good teacher," Anne Marie said.

"He's a pain in the ass."

"Sister said you're good for Sammy. She said you remind her of her little brother when they were kids. He got in a lot of trouble because of his ADD and some other head stuff and she was always trying to help him."

"No shit? What happened to him?" Conrad was interested in spite of himself.

"I think he died."

"Great." He stared at the grass awhile, then back at Anne Marie. "Why'd that judge send me to this shit hole?"

"He sends a lot of kids to Sister B. They're old friends."

"Yeah? But what's she doing out here in the jungle? She oughta' be in a church or something."

"Well, it's what she does. She's good at it. She sure helped *me* get it together."

"What?" Conrad pulled his eyes away from the stripes on Anne Marie's shirt and tried to concentrate.

"I said she helped *me*. I got sent here, too. Same judge. I've been coming back here as a counselor since I was seventeen, every summer break."

"You're shittin' me," he said.

"No, I'm not. The judge sent me here as kind of a last resort. He said if anyone could do anything with me, Sister B. could."

"What'd you get sent here for?"

Anne Marie's face turned red and she looked away. "I was on the streets."

"How on the streets?"

"You know."

"Oh." Conrad couldn't think of anything to say. He had seen plenty of girls on the street corners and in doorways, a lot of them no older than Sammy. But he couldn't picture Anne Marie like that.

"I guess you think I'm awful." She started to get up.

"No I don't." Conrad touched her arm. "I'm just surprised."

"If Sister B. can help me, she sure can help you."

"I don't need help," he said. "I just need to get back to my place."

In spite of his bravado, Conrad thought about what Anne Marie had said while he peeled the potatoes, and the carrots, and today apples for the pies the cook was going to bake. He estimated that in the last three weeks he had peeled 2100 potatoes and 1400 carrots. His plans to break out had been put aside until he could come up with a better strategy than the ones that had failed. Meanwhile he was getting used to all the mountain air and good food and most of all, Anne Marie. He kept reminding himself not to get too comfortable.

"You worked here long?" he asked the cook one afternoon in the middle of peeling yet more potatoes.

"Longer than you been alive," the cook said.

"What's your real name?" Conrad didn't really care but he was bored with the quiet.

"Cook."

"Yeah. Right. What is it really?"

"Cook. Elwood Cook." The man smiled, something unusual in Conrad's experience with him, and Conrad figured he was laughing at him.

"I got a question," Conrad said. "Why'd you rat on me about the booze?"

The cook shrugged and continued slicing the potatoes Conrad had peeled. Conrad turned his peeler over and over in his hand and then went back to peeling.

As the days turned into more weeks, and summer neared end, Conrad felt good. He'd put on weight and didn't look so much like a scarecrow. Sammy was learning his numbers, and losing some of his fat, saying he wanted to look more like Conrad. The kid wasn't so bad when he quit his bellyaching. Conrad used to do that kind of crap, too. He kept warning Sammy that you had to stay tough, keep on your toes when you're "out there." If they thought you were scared, you were dead meat.

"When we both leave here, can I come live with you?" Sammy asked him one evening when they had finished lessons and were tossing a ball around on the grass in front of the cabins.

Conrad had clapped him on the shoulder. He couldn't take Sammy back on the streets with him. Besides, the kid would have to go back home sooner or later.

"We'll see," he'd said vaguely, and resumed tossing the ball.

Anne Marie usually sat with him at meals. He didn't talk much but he liked her company. Now that he knew she wasn't some rich do-goodie girl volunteering at the camp, he felt easier around her. In fact he looked forward to these mealtimes with her. He could handle his time here as long as she was around.

Well into his third month at St. Phil's, Conrad's senses went on alert at dinner one evening when he saw the ominous expression on Sister Bernard's face. From his seat at the long table, he watched her survey the room like a prison guard. He felt those fierce blue eyes on him as they swept the dining room.

"We are missing some items from the office." The nun made the announcement as soon as the dishes had been cleared from the tables. "And some money. I believe I know what has happened to it, but I would like to give whoever is responsible a chance to return these items. You may bring them to me right after evening prayers." The nun turned and left the dining room, her back a ramrod, eyes looking to neither left nor right but straight ahead. Her Reeboks slapped the old beat-up wooden floor like a pair of Indian tom-toms.

"Shit. Shit. Shit," Conrad said under his breath. I knew it. Too good to be true. Ruined now. It's all ruined. Ex-con. Probation. It'll be me, they'll think I did it. Sister Bernard thinks I did it. I know she does. Why the fuck now! It was starting to work out. I even liked it here. Sort of.

His thoughts ran wild and turned to Anne Marie. Oh shit, Anne Marie, he thought. She'll blame me, too. I've gotta' get out of here. As soon as it gets dark. Head for Allentown, catch a ride, it's not that far, hole up for awhile. Maybe it's a frame. Maybe that goddam stool pigeon of a counselor. Look how the cook ratted on me!

As soon as it started to grow dark, he threw his extra shirt and jeans into his canvas bag and half-ran through the trees toward the highway. The whole time he expected to hear someone yell "Stop!" The whole scene reminded him of all the chases through dark alleys, down narrow back streets, some cop after him, waving a flashlight and screaming at him. He was winded and he needed to take a leak but he didn't dare stop.

He heard feet pounding behind him, branches snapping. Then heavy breathing, puffing. He crouched low. He could trip whoever it was and then run.

He groaned as a fat shape came out of the darkness and turned into Sammy.

"You're leaving!" Sammy hurled the accusation at him like a hard ball. "You can't leave. Not now!"

"Fuck, man, you scared the shit out of me! What the hell are you doing here?" Conrad's heart was pumping like he'd run a marathon.

Conrad remembered a night long ago, when he was about six, and his mother had packed them up and taken them to his aunt's house to stay, to get away from the old man. In the middle of the night he woke up to see his mother about to go out the door of the bedroom they were sharing, carrying her suitcase, and he had screamed the same thing at her..." You're leaving. Don't leave me here." But she had, for a while anyway.

"I got to go, kid," Conrad said, still trying to calm himself. "They're gonna lay this on *me*. I got to get away from here now while I can." He kicked at the dirt with his sneaker and punched the air. *Damn it, it was just getting good.*

Sammy started to sob. "I took the stuff, I done it, you gotta help me," the words all running together between sobs and hiccups.

Conrad balled his fists and wanted to punch the shit out of this sniveling brat. "What the fuck did you do that for?"

"I don't know." The kid sounded like he was being strangled. "I wanted to be like you. I thought maybe my mom...you know, would come up here and..."

Conrad flopped to the dirt in the middle of the road and Sammy sank down beside him, cross-legged, his head buried in his hands. "Take me along, please..."

Ah, Jesus, he thought. What the hell would he do with him? This dumb kid who didn't know shit from a bean pole. And why would this kid, or anyone else want to be like *him*, an all-time loser? He studied the pathetic-looking boy who sat crying beside him.

He supposed if Sammy could keep up, they could make Allentown before daylight, hole up somewhere til they got to his place. Him and Sammy. Dynamic duo. Sooner or later they'd make the kid go back to his parents. But maybe he could toughen him up before that. He'd have to find a way to feed them both. One thing for sure, he wasn't going to let Sammy get into the crap he'd been doing all his life.

"Come on," he said and yanked Sammy to his feet. "You have to keep up. And quit that sniveling. You gotta grow up now. You sure about this?"

Sammy nodded hard and wiped his nose with the back of his hand.

With every step along the dirt road, Conrad's doubts increased. It was one thing to teach this kid how to do arithmetic, but the thought of taking care of him out on the streets made him cringe. They had walked nearly a mile before Conrad realized it wasn't Sammy he was so much concerned about as himself.

"I'm tired of this shit." The words were out of his mouth before he realized he was thinking it and Sammy's head snapped up.

These last weeks were the first time he'd ever fit in anywhere besides the streets. And he was getting good at some stuff, like peeling potatoes and doing some cooking now. And Anne Marie said he was good at teaching. He pictured Anne Marie's big brown eyes and the smile that lit up her face. Even Sister Bernard had said he was helping Sammy. One thing about that old broad, she knew the score and you couldn't put anything over on her. She sure knew what to do with *him*.

"Come on, we're going back," he said.

"No..." Sammy pleaded. "They'll find out."

"We're gonna tell them." Conrad turned them both around and headed back the way they had come. He couldn't let the kid go down the tubes, pain in the ass that he was. He could square this with Sister Bernard. He knew he could. He'd get the numbers drilled into Sammy's head. That'd be part of the bargain if she let Sammy off. He knew how Sammy's brain worked, he'd show him how to get around all that stuff that messed with his head.

Sister Bernard was writing at one of the old work tables and looked up when Conrad pushed Sammy through the screen door. Conrad tried to gauge her expression but the old gal was hard to read sometimes. She looked up expectantly.

"We gotta talk to you, Sister," Conrad said, short of breath from nervousness.

"All right."

Conrad swallowed hard. This might be the biggest mistake of his life. He looked for the pencil holder and started to count… three, four, five…

"Well, what is it?" the nun said, not unkindly.

"I was getting out," Conrad said in a rush. He hadn't intended to tell her that. "I got out to the road. I figured everyone would think I took that stuff so I might as well clear out."

"So you were going to run away." She sounded really pissed again. Conrad began counting the drawers in filing cabinets along the wall…three, four, five…

"Conrad, look at me," Sister Bernard said. "You don't need to count. Look at me and tell me what happened."

How did she know he was counting? Half the time he didn't know it himself. He realized she had called him Conrad for the first time.

He didn't want to confess he'd been scared. Or that it mattered what the old nun thought of him. But next to his ma, she was the only person who'd ever cared what happened to him. "I knew you'd think I did it, what with my record and all."

"What brought you back?"

"I don't know." He felt like he was six years old again. He couldn't bring himself to say he wanted to stay. "It's okay here."

The nun nodded, looking satisfied. "I knew it wasn't you who took those items." She looked at Sammy then, eyebrows raised inquiringly.

Sammy was crying again. Conrad stepped close to him and laid a hand on the chubby shoulder.

"I took the stuff," the boy's words muffled.

"He'll give it all back, Sister. He just wanted his ma to come up here."

Sister Bernard looked from one to the other while Conrad held his breath.

"Bring the items to me now, Sammy," Sister Bernard said. She watched him run out the door and then she turned to Conrad. He braced himself.

"God works through his creatures," she said. "You were put in Sammy's life for a purpose. And apparently Sammy has been a gift to you."

Sammy a gift? In a rat's ass.

"I have hopes for you, Conrad," Sister Bernard went on.

Conrad's face felt hot. He felt a silly fuckin' grin on his face and he couldn't get it off. His eyes found the pencil holder on her desk and started counting. "Thanks."

"Thank you, *Sister.* And don't count, Conrad," she said. "I want you to look at me and pay attention. There are always consequences for our choices. And rewards. One often brings about the other."

What the hell was she talking about?

"You have broken yet another rule, even though you returned," she went on. "You must learn not to run away from your responsibilities and commitments. You are to move out of your cabin tonight…"

Conrad's heart sank. He looked down at his sneakers and in desperation began counting the eyelets that ran up the front… two, three, four…

"…and move into Sammy's cabin where you can help him and his cabin mates more with their lessons in preparation for school in the fall. And," she said, "toughen Sammy up a little before he goes home."

Conrad felt like she'd kicked him in the stomach. "Fix" Sammy. Teach a bunch of brats. *Some fuckin' consequences! Worse than getting sent back to jail.*

Sister Bernard pursed her lips. "You'll see the rewards one day," she said.

Anne Marie was sympathetic when he told her. They were sitting under the big tree where they met often these days. She was wearing a plain blue t-shirt so there were no stripes to count. Trying not to stare at her breasts, he counted the freckles splayed across her nose and cheeks…three, four, five…

"You'll do fine," she said. "You're a good teacher. A natural. I've seen you with Sammy."

"When do you leave?" He knew she was scheduled to go back to college soon, some school in Allentown, being paid for by whoever paid for St. Phil's. She wanted to be a social worker.

He felt down as he walked along the path toward the kitchen, where he was due to help Cook prepare dinner, knowing Anne Marie would be leaving soon. If she wasn't going to be here…well, he wished now he'd kept on going that night he'd started to run away.

He heard a loud thrashing through the bushes before he felt a hard bump against his side.

"Sammy! What the hell…"

"I'm going home!" Sammy yelled, loud and jubilant. "My mom's here. I've been looking for you, gotta' say goodbye."

"Good for you," was all Conrad could manage because he felt choked up all of a sudden. He'd actually miss the brat.

"Goddam good job," the cook said when Conrad walked into the kitchen and slipped on his cooking apron, first kind word Conrad had heard from the man. Pork tonight. Conrad could smell it roasting in the big oven.

If anyone had told Conrad back then that he would be teaching not one boy, not one small cabin full of rowdy boys, but *thirty* kids multiplications as well as higher level math like algebra, he would have scoffed, told them they were nuts. Yet here he was, in the comfort of his own home, leaning back in his desk chair, the latest batch of seventh grade algebra tests he'd been grading piled neatly on the desk.

The old judge who had sent him to St. Philomena's had died nearly three years ago. The Higher Ups had "retired" Sister Bernard two years later. He picked up a framed photograph of Sister Bernard, Anne Marie, and himself, standing in front of a church, Anne Marie with a corsage of white orchids on her shoulder and Conrad with a carnation in his jacket lapel.

Sammy was in college now. He called Conrad now and then when he was having a hard time with some of his courses, same ones that had stumped Conrad. He knew Sammy would make it eventually, the kid had developed guts. He glanced up at two diplomas hanging side by side on the wall, his and Anne Marie's. *If I can do it, anyone can.*

He replaced the photograph and made his way across the room to where a very pregnant woman sat dozing in an armchair, knitting needles and a ball of yarn forgotten in her lap.

"Care for a short walk, Mrs. Shaltzhammer? "

Anne Marie woke with a start. She laid aside the tiny blue sweater she was knitting and smiled as Conrad pulled her up from the chair. He kissed her soundly and began counting the freckles that played across her nose…three, four, five, six…

The Four-Poster

There was no reply from the bed, but Eleanor was used to the silence. She hadn't heard her husband's voice in months. The stroke had taken away his ability to speak.

She set down the breakfast tray and made her voice light and cheery to cover up her weariness. "I boiled you an egg. And here's coffee." She breathed in the aroma and wished she had remembered to bring some for herself. She would pour a cup when she went back downstairs.

She pulled a chair close to the high four-poster bed, a wedding gift more than sixty years ago. The September sunlight slanted across flowered wallpaper and a tall Victorian mahogany dresser. It fell on a framed snapshot of a young man sitting on the steps of a porch, laughing into the camera. *Nathaniel.* She loved his name. Like a poet's, or a statesman's. Usually she called him "Nattie" but not all the time, she so enjoyed saying "Nathaniel" and feeling the "a's" and the "th's."

"The children are coming by later," she said. She suspected what they were up to, but she did not want to upset her husband and so did not elaborate. Instead, she smoothed the folds in the heavy quilt of flowers and wreaths that she and her twin sisters had sewn long ago in the months before her wedding. She no longer noticed the faded colors or the holes she had patched over the years. How many times had her daughter told her to get rid of it! "Get a decent cover," Carrie kept saying. But that would be giving up a little corner of her life.

After awhile she made her way back down the stairs, clinging to the railing and favoring her left hip. She could smell something burning and she hurried as quickly as she was able toward the kitchen.

"Oh, dear," she sighed, pushing a scorched pan off the lighted stove burner…the pan she had boiled his egg in. She should have had Mrs. McCoy do it. But she liked to make Nathaniel's breakfast herself. She opened a window to try to get rid of the odor and carried the ruined pan to the back porch, where she buried it in a trash container. She would ask Mrs. McCoy to get rid of it when she came in later to help her. Better if Carrie and John didn't know.

Lowering herself onto one of the tall-backed wooden chairs at the kitchen table, she gazed at the row of cupboards that lined the walls. So much of their life was stacked on the shelves behind those cupboard doors. They had lived in this same house since they were first married. When Carrie and John had been home… she still thought of this as their home…she had used everything. The china plates and saucers, the Christmas angels and the ceramic snowmen that the children had given her, tarnished silver trays from her mother's own home. The heart-shaped cake pans. The old potato masher. She had loved cooking big dinners for her family. Always a crowd at the table, Carrie's and John's friends, their cousins, her parents and twin sisters, Nathaniel's mother and ancient grandmother. Grandmother Carolyn had been almost ninety, and here she was, nearly that herself. The old folks all gone now, her family and Nathaniel's family both. Even her sisters. She missed them all.

She heard the car in the driveway and realized how much time had elapsed. It was nearly noon. The children were here. Maybe they would stay long enough to have lunch with her.

Carrie came into the kitchen first, her presence seeming to take up a great deal of space in the room. She was tall, like her father. She dyed her hair a reddish brown that Eleanor didn't much care for, but it made Carrie look younger than her sixty-five years. Which, Eleanor supposed, was what everyone wanted these days.

John followed his sister into the kitchen, older than Carrie by four years but not nearly so imposing. His hair was completely gray now and thin on top. It was hard to see them as grown. More than just grown. Lines and creases in their faces, Carrie with her thickened body, John slumped a little through his shoulders, like Nathaniel, walking stiffly because of his bad back.

Carrie crossed to her mother and pecked at her cheek. "Hello, Mother," she said. She sniffed the air and glanced at the stove. "Did you burn something?"

"No." Eleanor looked away from her daughter, not meeting her eyes.

John bent to embrace her and held his cheek against hers for a moment. He eased himself into a chair beside her.

"We have some pictures to show you." Carrie pulled a bundle of glossy pamphlets from her purse.

"What are they?" Eleanor asked, although she suspected. "Are they of the children? I haven't seen them for so long." Carrie and John each had a boy and a girl, out on their own now. In her mind she saw her children as young parents, holding important jobs. And now they were retired. Where had all those years gone?

"…very nice apartments," Carrie was saying. "Where you can take some of your furniture with you and be with other people your age, and not have to live on your own in this big old house." Carrie spread the pamphlets fan-like in front of her mother.

"But I'm not on my own," Eleanor protested. "Your father and I…"

John placed a hand over his mother's thin fluttering fingers. "A good place for both of you," he said. "Where Dad can get the best of care." He gave his sister a warning look.

"Don't you want to go up and see your father?" Eleanor wanted to turn the talk away from apartments and nursing homes.

"Maybe later," John said.

"Was Mrs. McCoy here this morning?" Carrie continued sniffing the air and looked dubious.

"Oh yes," Eleanor nodded. "She'll be back soon." She hated lying to Carrie. And she hated another woman looking after her house.

Eleanor stared at the pictures in the brochures. Modern-looking rooms with curved couches and fat lamps and carpets like those in Good Housekeeping advertisements. Bedrooms with shiny spreads and narrow bureaus. Small kitchens, really just little alcoves, with no sign of pans or dishes. Pictures of lounges filled with men in V-necked sweaters and women in pretty matched outfits, all of them with full heads of beautiful white hair, laughing, playing cards, sipping drinks from tall glasses, having the best time.

"No nursing home," she said flatly, and pushed the pamphlets away.

Later Eleanor climbed the stairs and examined the breakfast tray beside the bed.

"You haven't eaten a thing," she scolded. Carrie and John had left without staying for lunch and this time she had been glad to see them go. All that talk about apartments and retirement places. Pushing and pulling her. They hadn't even gone upstairs to see their father.

"They want to put us in a nursing home. Carrie and John," she said. "They think I can't take care of you any longer."

She walked around to her side of the bed and, with an effort, raised herself onto the high mattress. She longed to hear his voice. It had been the best baritone in the choir at Holy Angels. The house seemed so quiet and empty now without the sound of it.

"Do you remember the first time we met?" She lay on her back staring at the tall carved posts at the bottom of the bed. "At the festival at Holy Angels. I had turned twenty-one just two weeks before, and you were already a businessman, a college graduate, imagine. I heard you laughing and I thought you had the most wonderful voice I'd ever heard." She smiled at the memory.

"You bumped into me and made me splash punch all over my dress. My dress with the rose-colored sash. And you kept saying how sorry you were, but all the while you couldn't stop laughing. Because I was so upset about my dress. And you made me laugh after a while, too."

She rolled onto her side. "I barely came up to your shoulder," she said. "And your eyes…you always squeezed them shut when you laughed." Her own eyes burned with the start of tears.

"Oh, Nattie, you were so handsome. I've loved you so." She gazed longingly across the room at the photograph of the young man on the dresser. "I wish we could be young and beautiful again."

She lay still, lost in her thoughts.

"Do you remember how beautiful Holy Angels looked on our wedding day, with all the spring flowers and the candles burning on the altar?" she said after awhile. "My father shook so hard going down the aisle that he had to hold onto me all the way. And I walked like this…take a step, pause, then another step, pause…" As she spoke, she moved her shoulders in rhythm to the remembered bridal walk, her hands wrapped around an imaginary bouquet of roses and ivy.

"I could feel my gown swishing around my legs every time I moved." She laughed softly. "My veil made everything seem blurred and when I looked at you waiting at the end of the aisle, it was as though a lovely cloud enveloped your whole body."

The ringing of the telephone startled Eleanor out of her reverie. Her hand trembled as she reached for the phone next to the bed.

"Mother, I've made an appointment for us to look at one of those apartments tomorrow," Carrie said without preamble.

Eleanor felt dizzy. "Oh my…" she breathed into the phone.

"Now listen, Mother. John and I will pick you up at nine o'clock in the morning. You'll be ready, won't you?"

"I…don't…know. Your father…"

"He'll be fine," Carrie said impatiently. "Mrs. McCoy will be there. And Mother, well, let Mrs. McCoy cook your dinner tonight. Stay away from the stove."

Eleanor murmured goodbye and lay down on the high bed once more. "Carrie is so short-tempered with me these days. Maybe it will be a relief to her to put us away somewhere," she said.

She lay quietly in the stillness. Summertime noises drifted through a window. Someone was mowing grass nearby. She recognized the chatter of sparrows in the tree next to the house. She liked these familiar sounds. They comforted her when she felt lonely for Nathaniel's voice.

"You know I would do anything to help you, Nattie," she said after awhile. "If a nursing home would be good for you…but I don't want to leave here."

Nathaniel seemed so far away from her today. If only he could tell her what to do. She had no idea how she would organize herself to pack up the house and move. It was hard to concentrate. Starting in on one job and then, before she knew it, she'd be trying to remember what it was she was doing.

"I'm going to fix us some chops for dinner," she said. She had remembered to take them out of the freezer after Carrie and John left, proof that she wasn't as disorganized as the children believed.

"This is one of our nicest apartments," the young woman was saying the next morning. She was not much older than Carrie's daughter, Eleanor thought. Attractive in her peach-colored dress with the pretty hummingbird pin on the collar. Lorraine, that was her name. She would try to remember it.

Lorraine was leading them into a small living room with a couch upholstered in big cabbage roses and two bright yellow chairs, each with a miniature table at arm's reach.

Eleanor thought longingly of her pale green mohair couch, three times re-upholstered after hours of poring over big books filled with fabric samples. And their four-poster…she hurried across the beige carpet and into a bedroom furnished with a dresser, a leather arm chair, and a narrow bed covered with a flowered cotton spread.

"Will our bed fit?"

Lorraine looked at Carrie and John before replying. "You need to have this type of bed so that it can be raised and lowered. In case of illness…"

"But what about Nathaniel? There's no room here for two beds," Eleanor said.

Their young guide started to speak but Carrie held up a hand to stop her and steered her mother back into the living room and onto the flowered couch. "Dad may have to stay in the hospital wing for now," she said. Her tone was gentler than usual.

Eleanor heard this as though from a distance. She looked questioningly at Lorraine, saw a moment's uncertainty cross the younger woman's face.

"You could visit him," Lorraine rallied, her voice lifting cheerily, a chirp.

Visit him?

Eleanor allowed them to lead her back through the bedroom to a tiled bath, where the commode was raised high up off the floor between two stainless steel bars, like fences. A shower stall took up one end of the room and it, too, was full of shiny bars and handles.

"These are for safety," Lorraine was saying. "And here is a buzzer to push when you want an aide to come to help you."

Eleanor backed away in dismay and retraced her steps into the living room. A buzzer, an aide to help her in the bathroom?

"The kitchen?" Her throat felt tight. Lorraine had forgotten to show them the kitchen.

"You'll be able to eat all your meals in the dining room," Lorraine said. "You won't have to cook ever again!"

Later, Eleanor stood by the bed and fussed with the quilt, smoothing and patting and rubbing the trails of tiny stitches. Much of the furniture downstairs would be carted off to an auction house, the things John and Carrie and the grandchildren didn't want to keep. She looked around the room. If only they would allow her to take their bed along. John had been born in this bed. She had gone to the hospital to have Carrie, but John had come into the world right here. Now the bed would belong to her granddaughter, to Carrie's girl, and it would sit in some modern apartment, out of place.

"The children will be here to get us any minute now," she said. She didn't want to alarm Nathaniel about the bed, so she didn't tell him they could not take it. Stiffly, she stretched out on the bed. She had put on her best navy blue dress with the white collar and she had laid out Nathaniel's favorite tan sport coat and a pair of slacks. She smoothed out the skirt of her dress, trying not to wrinkle it.

"I can stand anything as long as we're together," she said. "But they're going to put us in different rooms. I'm afraid, Nattie." She wiped away a tear that slipped down her cheek. "I wish we didn't have to go."

Maybe she should refuse to leave. Insist that Carrie hire someone to come in and help Mrs. McCoy. But Carrie had said that wouldn't be enough. Carrie and John both said they needed to be cared for all the time.

She thought about the pills the doctor had given to her after Nathaniel had his stroke. They all thought she needed something "to get through." But she never took them. She could use the pills now for both of them. Just mix them in a glass of juice. They could stay together that way. She tried to decide what would be the best thing to do.

"You're my life," she whispered. "I would do anything for you. Even that."

She sat up and tried to remember where she had put the pills. But it was too late. Carrie and John were already opening the front door. She had waited too long. She slid her legs over the side of the bed, holding on to the edge until she regained her balance. Her fingers lingered against the quilt and trailed over the mahogany bedpost.

Carrie strode into the room, followed by John, both pairs of eyes taking in the untouched breakfast tray, the smoothed-out quilt tucked tightly under the edges of the mattress. Carrie's glance fell on her father's tan jacket and his old brown slacks draped over the armchair by the window. She placed a hand on her mother's arm, but Eleanor shrugged it off and walked toward the door.

"Help your father to dress, John," Eleanor said over her shoulder. A flash of anger gave strength to her voice. "His clothes are right there." They had wanted to get rid of all his clothes but she had not allowed it.

She turned back and saw John move to the mahogany dresser, where he lifted the picture of the young man on the porch steps. He touched the face with a trembling finger and then held the picture out to her. "Don't you want to take this along?" he asked.

She took the picture in both hands and looked around the room, the last time, she knew. The bed seemed strangely flat to her. No long, lean form rumpling the lines of the quilt. Nathaniel must have gone on ahead of her. He must have gone out with Carrie. But no, Carrie was still here, right beside her. He must have slipped out while she wasn't looking. She'd have to hurry, not keep him waiting. He so hated to be away from her. She held the photograph against her chest and made her way carefully down the stairs.

The Contest Winner

The baby had no name of his own so she called him Jakey. The mother had walked out of the hospital and disappeared the day after he was born. He had trouble breathing and there was a heart problem.

"Will he live?" Rena Mary asked the first time she saw Jakey.

"I doubt it, but who knows?" Nurse Atkins told her.

After her early morning visit with Jakey, Rena Mary took an elevator to the housekeeping department on the lower level of the hospital and collected her cleaning supplies. The heel of her white sneaker was rubbing and she bent to tug at her sock. She wore tan pants, as always, and a loose fitting t-shirt with a sailboat on the front. It had caught her eye in one of the crammed full racks at the thrift shop she liked to peruse for an occasional purchase.

With her sneaker readjusted and her heel relieved of the pressure, she took the elevator to the fourth floor. She pushed her mop into Room 402 West, Mrs. Langley's room, gathering all the dust balls into a pile on the linoleum.

"What's a six-letter word that starts with 'h' and means 'kind,' the third letter is 'm?'" the old woman asked. Without pausing in her mopping, Rena Mary said "humane."

"Yes, that fits." Mrs. Langley penciled in the missing letters. Rena Mary knew Mrs. Langley was in her seventies and had five grandchildren. She was propped up in bed with pillows behind her, a pale blue bed jacket across her shoulders, her white hair piled on top of her head in a loose bun. She was undergoing tests.

Rena Mary prolonged the mopping and dusting. She liked cleaning in Mrs. Langley's room. The old woman talked to her as though she were a real person and not an extension of her mop.

At Mrs. Langley's suggestion, Rena Mary had entered a crossword puzzle contest that the local newspaper was sponsoring.

"You're an expert, I'm sure you will win a prize," Mrs. Langley said.

Twelve persons who completed all the puzzles for two weeks... especially difficult puzzles...would receive $200 each. Not only that, they would be guests at a special luncheon. Rena Mary had mailed in a completed puzzle each day and waited for the newspaper to announce the winners.

She finished Mrs. Langley's room and the other Fourth Floor rooms assigned to her and at three o'clock she stored her mop and bucket and dust cloths in the housekeeping closet next to the laundry. She hurried up a flight of stairs to the nursery.

"Maybe I'll win," she said to Jakey and the baby made a small gurgling sound.

She thought about the baby during the bus ride home and while she heated beef stew for her supper. She had brought home the morning newspaper from the lobby and began the day's crossword puzzle while she ate. A unit of light, four letters, begins with "p." She thought of "phot," saw that it worked. The next word was more difficult...a Chinese puzzle. "Tangram" came into her head and she wrote it in. She never knew how these words came to her.

She laid down the paper and boiled some water for tea, something she liked to do in the evening. She saw important women drink tea in old television movies. She especially liked Miss Jane Marple's teatimes in the Agatha Christie movies. Miss Marple was so smart. And very important in her English village. Rena Mary wondered what it would be like to be important, to have friends call up and say, "Come on over," or "Let's meet for lunch tomorrow."

On the day the contest winners were to be announced, Rena Mary went to work a little earlier than usual so that she could stop by the lobby and look at the morning paper. The young woman at the switchboard raised a thumb in salute and held the paper out to her. The headline..."12 Winners Announced in Puzzle Contest"...appeared in a small box at the bottom of the front page. And then their names...*her name*...and the notice that they would be honored at a luncheon the following Wednesday at the Elks Club.

Rena Mary sat down on one of the plastic lobby seats. Her breath came in short sharp jerks. She couldn't control the grin that stretched so wide that her cheeks began to ache. She hugged herself and rocked back and forth in the seat.

"Jakey, I won," she whispered a few minutes later, bending over the small crib in the Second Floor nursery. The baby made his bleating lamb's cries, his tiny body trembling with the effort.

"Hush, baby, I'm right here," Rena Mary murmured. With a gloved hand she gently stroked the infant's stomach and then his face under the miniscule oxygen tube, caressed his little hands that waved aimlessly. The baby quieted and dropped off to sleep.

"I'll be back," Rena Mary promised.

By the end of the week Rena Mary had become a celebrity. Her supervisor pasted the newspaper story on the bulletin board in the housekeeping office. Mrs. Langley, still undergoing tests, had taped the article to the door of her closet. On Friday, one of the maids brought in a chocolate layer cake and the women had a party during their lunch hour, with ham sandwiches and potato salad and the cake. Rena Mary sat at a fold-out table between two of the other maids, eating a sandwich and listening to the chatter. *What would it be like to do this every day?*

At three o'clock, she put away her cleaning equipment and took the elevator to the nursery. She described the newspaper story and the special awards lunch to Jakey, and told him about the chocolate cake the maids had brought for her. The baby's skin seemed paler, she thought, and his fingernails more bluish. She asked Nurse Atkins about it.

"He has more fluid buildup," the nurse said, her voice calm although her green eyes looked worried. Rena Mary wished she could be tall and pretty like Nurse Atkins, instead of so plain.

"If anything should happen..." she whispered.

"Would you like me to call you?"

Rena Mary wrote down her phone number.

She had taken off work the day of the luncheon. She had been up since daybreak, too nervous to eat her usual bowl of cereal, just having coffee and toast. She dusted the furniture in the living room, vacuumed the carpet, and wiped up the kitchen floor.

Finally, when it was almost nine o'clock, and she couldn't think of anything else to do, she began to dress. Her pantyhose felt foreign against her legs after wearing cotton socks every day. She pulled on a flowered skirt and buttoned up a white blouse. She was tying back her hair when the phone rang.

"This is Susan Atkins." It took Rena Mary a second to realize it was Nurse Atkins from the hospital.

"Your little friend is in trouble," the nurse said. "Would you like to come in?"

"To say goodbye?" Rena Mary's voice sounded raspy to her own ears.

"Probably," the nurse said.

She tried to hold back tears as she caught the nine-thirty bus. She willed it to go faster. She wanted to be there, hold Jakey's tiny hand when…

The oxygen mask covered the baby's face almost completely, only the top of his little forehead was showing. Heart pounding, Rena Mary quickly washed her hands and pulled a gown over her skirt and blouse. She yanked on long gloves that stretched to her elbows. She glanced at the large round clock on the wall above the sink…ten-fifteen.

"It could be any time now," Nurse Atkins said. She was studying charts with an eye on her tiny patient.

Rena Mary sat down on a hard plastic chair beside the crib. She felt calmer now that she was here next to Jakey. She wished she could have stayed close like this to her own boy. The baby's skin looked blue. It seemed to her she could almost see through it.

"Don't you have your luncheon today?" Nurse Atkins asked after a while.

Rena Mary looked at the clock again. It was just after eleven. She calculated the time it would take to walk from the hospital to the Elks Club. If she left the hospital at eleven-thirty, or even a few minutes later, she could make it by noon.

"I have time," she said, aware of a whisper-like touch on her gloved finger. She leaned in closer and hummed a tune from her childhood. She used to hum the same song to Joey. The baby's grasp on her finger quivered and settled. Rena Mary could just barely see his eyes under the mask…she wished he would open them and see her. She wanted him to know she was there with him.

Nurse Atkins' voice startled her. "It's nearly noon, don't you need to go? You're going to be late and miss everything."

She could just make it if she walked fast. She straightened her back and started to get up. It wouldn't matter if she was a little late for the luncheon, just so she was there to hear her name called out. She pictured standing with the other contest winners, walking to the front of the room and being introduced, accepting her prize. Her name spoken in a room full of people. She looked down at the baby.

Why now? He's hung on all week, why now?

The flash of anger shocked her. "I'll come right back," she whispered to the baby. "I'll only be an hour or two." An hour to feel important. "Hold on, just a little longer," she said.

She felt a light pressure on her finger again. The baby's tiny legs stiffened. *What must it be like to be so small and all alone and dying?* Like her own boy had been.

She looked up at the clock on the wall and as though in one of her puzzles, the word "inevitable" ran through her mind. Her life was inevitable. She settled back down onto the hard chair.

With her thumb and index finger, she massaged the bird-like feet and restless hands, and gently stroked the little stomach. She kneaded the fragile legs until they relaxed and caressed the tiny wrinkled forehead above the mask, feeling a pulse twitch faintly at the temple. With her other hand, she rubbed the small of her own back, which ached from the hours of sitting bent over the crib. After awhile, the feathery touch against her finger stopped. The infant's hands were quiet now and his arms fell to the sides of his body. The little chest was still.

Rena Mary lifted one tiny hand and held it a while longer before she laid it down. She continued to gaze at the small form. She felt a touch on her shoulder and looked up to see Nurse Atkins beside her.

"He never really had a chance," the nurse said.

Rena Mary felt old and tired when she finally stood up. She saw by the wall clock that it was nearly 2 o'clock.

She took an elevator to the fourth floor and walked into Mrs. Langley's room, grateful the old woman was still there. Mrs. Langley listened and nodded, patted Rena Mary's hand. After awhile, Rena Mary wiped her eyes and blew her nose, told Mrs. Langley she was all right.

Rena Mary solemnly mopped the dust balls from the corners of Room 402 West the next day. Mrs. Langley had gone home. She hadn't had a chance to say goodbye. An old man with an oxygen tube wound across his cheeks dozed in the bed now, snoring in spastic stops and starts. Rena Mary finished dusting the room in silence and moved on. At three o'clock, she stored her supplies in the housekeeping closet and took an elevator to the lobby. She nodded at the young woman at the switchboard as she tucked the morning newspaper under her arm.

The bus was on schedule. She climbed aboard and stared out the window, seeing the tiny face in the darkened glass again, like the day before. Not until the bus reached her stop did she pull her eyes away. Then she climbed off the bus and went home.

BREAKTHROUGH

*A*rthur spotted Midge Ryder right away. She was about five feet tall, eyes half hidden by frizzy red hair, and the only female in the yard smoking a cigar. In this case, one of those long skinny panatelas. She leaned against the shoulder-high stone wall that edged the grass compound and scowled at him as he approached.

"You must be Midge." He told her his name.

"They took my fuckin' shoe laces." She flung the words at him, cigar fumes pouring from her mouth.

"They don't want you to hang yourself with them." Arthur used his nice guy welcoming smile.

"So what're you in here for, Lard Ass?" She stared at Arthur's ample mid-section and the size 42 chinos stretched across it.

"I work here."

She shrugged. "Big fuckin' deal," she said. She turned her back on him and headed for the opposite side of the yard, where she squatted on the grass and puffed on the cigar.

Arthur smiled. He was used to the unexpected here, even trash-mouthed girls who looked like leprechauns. After all, it was a psychiatric hospital. The juvenile nuthouse, his friends chided.

He really liked the patients here, these kids who seemed so out of sync with the world.

Later, after Midge and the other patients had wandered back inside the building, Arthur tapped lightly on the door of 60 East. He liked this part of his job the best…getting to know a new patient. He liked to hear their stories, hear what had happened to them that they ended up here. Some of them talked about it. Some clammed up right at the beginning and stayed that way. He wasn't sure which Marjorie Kathleen Ryder, aka Midge, would do.

She was sitting on the edge of her bed staring at something she held in her hands. A stuffed bear rested against a pillow at the head of the bed, dressed in a small sweater with MacDonald stitched across the front. Years of rubbing had darkened and matted its brown fur. The girl herself wore jeans, like most of the kids here, and a baggy gray sweatshirt. Plaid lace-less sneakers fell half off her feet. Her red hair needed combing and sunlight from the window bounced off it like static electricity. She looked like a child, although Arthur knew from her chart that she was sixteen.

The girl held a small stone, almost perfectly round in shape, about the size of a quarter, its steel-gray sheen like polished pewter. She opened her hand wide and lifted it toward him. Smiling. He had seen the same smile on other patients, ones in the throes of some delusion, or close to mania.

"Smell it," she commanded. "Smell the sulphur."

He lifted the stone out of the palm of her hand and sniffed. It smelled like sweat. He shrugged.

"Where'd you get it?"

"It's from hell," she said. She blinked at him, her face carefully blank. "It's an alien. From hell."

He put the stone back into her hand. "Nice. You have group therapy in ten minutes. Want me to walk you down?"

She pushed her feet all the way into the plaid sneakers and stood up. "Know why I'm here?" she said, that smile on her face again.

Arthur hoped she would confide, start to establish a bond.

"I'm a sociopath. No conscience." She crossed her arms in smug satisfaction.

Arthur thought about the smile. It could be true.

"I saw a kid ride his bike into a sewer. This big hole in the ground. Rode it in like some freakin' rodeo clown." She lowered her head and looked up at him through the red frizz that fell over her forehead and into her eyes. "He didn't come back out."

Arthur didn't really believe her. "What did you do?" he asked.

"Nothin'. Oh yeah, I clapped. It was a good show. Stupid kid."

Then Arthur remembered reading something about an eight-year-old boy who had drowned in an open sewer a while back. He looked at the girl more closely.

"Why did they put you here?"

"They think I'm crazy."

"Are you?"

"Fuckin' A." She walked past him and out into the corridor, the heels of her plaid sneakers slapping on the linoleum. He followed her down the hallway to the therapy room and waited until she disappeared through the door.

The following afternoon, with an hour to kill before he left for work, Arthur roamed around his little kitchen, grabbing the knob of the wall pantry where he kept snacks, then whipping his hand off the knob like it was a hot flame. He moved to the sink, poured a glass of water from the tap and stared out the window at his garden. The garden and patio were the best part of his townhouse. You'd never know you were so close to the city when you were outside in the midst of all the plants and flowers.

He caught sight of his reflection in the window glass.

I should be out walking. I should be out running! He needed to get rid of about thirty pounds he had put on in the last year since Connie took off for Arizona with their kick-box instructor. That's when he had started stuffing himself with whatever fell into his hands. Tastykakes did the most for him. He bought them by the case. The chocolate crème-filled cupcakes were his favorite. But any would do----Krimpets, Honey Buns, the little round coffee cakes…

"They're loaded with cholesterol," warned the other nurses when they spotted them in his locker. "Look at this!" they'd say, grabbing a pack of crème-filled Koffee Kakes and waving them in his face. "Two-hundred and forty calories in these two babies! And 30 mg's of cholesterol! You're clogging all your arteries, Arthur."

He didn't care. Well, he cared. Who wanted to have a heart attack. But he couldn't seem to help himself. He and Connie had shared the townhouse for three years and had finally committed to a wedding date when she took off. He couldn't figure out why she had left him. They'd been so well matched. They both enjoyed the gardening, and cooking Italian food, which they did every Friday evening, and watching movies on HBO, an extravagance Arthur had added to the cable package. One he probably should cancel now.

Before he could stop himself he had swung back across the kitchen, opened the pantry door and grabbed a handful of cellophane-wrapped chocolate crème-filled cupcakes with butter cream icing striped with chocolate. He bit one in half and chewed with relief. He felt better already. He carried the rest of the carton out onto the patio, where he flopped on a webbed lawn chair and devoured the remainder of the cakes. Chewing, he watched a pair of wrens go in and out of the small birdhouse he had hung in his pink dogwood and wished Connie were here.

Arthur had the following weekend off, and weekends were always tough on new patients. When he wasn't answering phone calls from one of the nurses relaying angry messages from Midge, he worked in his yard, watering and clipping the flowers he'd planted in small beds and big clay pots positioned around the postage-stamp patio. His neighbors had copied his garden. They had discussed the plantings with him and then arranged their own yards and patios as close to his layout as they could…planters filled with impatiens, geraniums, daisies, blue delphinium. A dogwood. Little white trellises with climbing pink and coral tea roses. He was especially fond of the bamboo trees he had planted at the far edge of the yard, near the fence, blocking off any view from the side street. Most of his neighbors had planted bamboo along their fences, too.

"Midge left you another note," Annabelle, his favorite on the nursing staff, said on the phone.

"Read it to me, will you." Arthur knew the numerous ways Midge might raise cane about his not being there.

"'Arthur, you are a total shit!'" Annabelle read to him. "'I really wanted to talk to you today. It's important. And you didn't show up. If I had my shoe laces, I'd use them. I've already filed a complaint. You'd better have a fucking good explanation for deserting me.'" Annabelle made clucking sounds through the phone.

Arthur thought awhile about an answer. This might be some kind of breakthrough. He called Annabelle back and asked her to give Midge a message: "Dear Midge, I'm not deserting you. I'll be back soon. If you want to talk to someone else right now, talk to Saul. He's a nice guy. Arthur."

The reply came that evening: "Arthur, screw you. And Saul and everyone else in this God-forsaken place. Who needs you? Anyway, I think I'll be leaving in another day. Sayonara."

"Dear Midge," he replied. "I checked it out and you're not really leaving. I found a nice dish garden to put your stone in. I hope you'll stick around until Monday. I'll bring it to you."

"Arthur---shove it."

Carrying a dish garden of non-breakable plastic, Arthur tapped on Midge's door the following Monday. The room was empty and MacDonald was not in his usual place against the pillow at the head of Midge's bed. Something hung from the top of the window blind. Arthur moved farther into the room and saw that it was MacDonald, a shoelace knotted into a noose around his neck and hooked over the top of the blind. The bear swung in tiny circles, caught in the draft from the corridor.

Arthur looked to see whether Midge had left a note to accompany the hanging, but there was only the small round stone on the bedside table. He placed the flower-filled dish garden beside it.

He found her in the television room at one of the game tables, systematically ripping the morning newspaper into shreds. She kept her eyes fixed on her handiwork. He slid into a chair across the table from her.

"Nice work. You could get a job with the government shredding secret documents."

She made no reply.

"How come you hung MacDonald?"

"He fuckin' needed hanging," she mumbled.

"Where'd you get a shoe lace to hang him with?"

A look of triumph replaced the scowl on her face. "Well, Fats, that's for me to know. So fuck off."

Arthur made no move to get up. "I put a dish garden in your room for you. To put your stone in. It has some moss and violets in it."

She grimaced. "Good, I can break it up in little pieces and slit my freakin' wrists."

"It's plastic, you can't," Arthur said.

She shoved the paper shreds onto the floor, creating a waterfall of black and white newsprint, and stomped out. Arthur knew she was headed back to her room to see the dish garden.

He pushed his tray along the hospital cafeteria line, picking up three pork chops, a large scoop of mashed potatoes, a small spoonful of green beans for nutritional value, and a couple of chocolate chip muffins. He spooned pork gravy over his potatoes, and as an after-thought, dripped some over the chops. He added a small dish of applesauce and, reluctantly, a bowl of tossed salad. This he smothered with bleu cheese dressing and topped with a heap of bacon bits. His stomach growled and he could hardly wait to find a table and start eating.

He was cutting up a chop when Twila Ashley, Midge's therapist, set her tray down close to his and slid into a chair across from him.

"Mind?" she asked.

Arthur liked Twila. She was probably too old for him, in her thirties somewhere, but if there had been no Connie, well who knew? She had pretty brown hair, like Connie's, and big green eyes and a sexy mouth that he couldn't take his eyes from. She achieved good results with most of her patients, too, and Arthur was glad Midge had been assigned to her.

"About Midge Ryder," Twila said, biting into a pizza slice and rolling the hot cheese around in her mouth with obvious pleasure. Twila enjoyed food as much as Arthur did, which was one of the reasons he liked sharing a table with her at dinner. Lucky for her, she was thin as a rail and could eat anything she wanted without gaining an ounce. It's all in the metabolism, he told himself.

"She likes you, you know," Twila said after she had swallowed. "Well, maybe you don't know. It's hard to tell if Midge likes you. She can be pretty crusty."

Arthur laughed involuntarily. *Crusty!* "She's got a mouth on her like a stevedore."

"I know, she's hard to take. But the fact is, she does like you and I think she trusts you. She told me about the dish garden you brought her. And the way you arranged the flowers so she could put her stone in the center. That was a nice thing to do. Inspirational."

Arthur shrugged. Let Twila think he was brilliant, what the heck. Dish gardens, flowers, planting stuff…all second nature to him.

Arthur cut up his third pork chop.

"Midge has a personality disorder, you know," Twila went on.

This didn't surprise Arthur. Who didn't have a personality disorder when you got right down to it? He and Connie used to spend hours trying to find themselves in the latest edition of the DSM, the psychiatric Diagnostics & Statistical Manual that lists the required number of symptoms a person needs to qualify as bonkers. (*Fill in the number*) *out of the following* (*fill in*) *symptoms to indicate* (*fill in the blanks*) and so forth, depending on what year it was.

"She's not a sociopath like Dr. M. thought at first. She's a borderline." Twila's tone was hushed the way people talk in a mortuary.

Arthur never had believed Midge was a sociopath, in spite of all her efforts to convince him otherwise. She wasn't charming enough for a sociopath. He was sorry to hear about the "borderline" thing though. Time bombs, the staff called them. Misinterpreted your every word and gesture, got violent sometimes. On the other hand, he also knew that some of the shrinks diagnosed "borderline" when they couldn't figure out what the heck was wrong with a patient. Hopefully this was the case with Midge.

"My problem is, I can't get her to do anything productive in group therapy sessions," Twila said. "She tends to disrupt the group. She has a way about her…"

"What exactly do you want me to do?" he asked.

"See if you can find a way to motivate her."

Arthur came up with the deal a few days later. He was thinning out the daisies in his garden, talking to himself, or rather to the daisies, as he worked.

"You'll see, thinning is good for you," he told the blossoms. "I wish someone would thin me out as easy as this."

Lard Ass, he heard inside his head, where Midge's sardonic expression floated often these days. That's when the plan came to him.

Midge was in the hospital yard puffing on one of her panatelas when he arrived at work that afternoon. She pretended not to see him when he strolled toward her across the grass.

"About your group therapy. I'll make a deal with you," he said, fanning away the cloud of cigar fumes she aimed in his direction. "Where in the heck do you get these cigars, anyway?"

She glared at him and blew more smoke toward his face, the breeze and bright sunlight playing havoc with her unruly hair.

"Fats, there's nothing you can do to make me talk about anything in that freakin' group. Forget it." She tried to move past him but he blocked her path.

"Wait! You'll like this. It's a plan. Just listen. If you'll start working in group, I'll go on a diet and lose weight."

"Screw you," she said. But she stood still and looked hard at his waistline.

"You start working, I quit eating," he said.

Silence.

"Every time you go to group therapy and talk about your stuff, I'll lose some poundage."

She hooted and walked away. She reached the opposite side of the yard, swung around and came back to where Arthur stood waiting. "This I gotta' see," she said.

The cafeteria gradually filled up with hospital staff and frazzled-looking visitors. Arthur made his way without enthusiasm along the food line, picking up a chicken breast, grilled, no breading. A green salad. A cup of canned fruit cocktail. He wavered as he slid the tray past the desserts. The cooks had baked one of his favorites today, chocolate cake with peanut butter icing. He hurriedly swept the tray along toward an empty table, as far away as possible from the aroma coming from the steam tables in the cafeteria line. It had been nearly three weeks and it was only now starting to get easier.

Twila set her tray on the table across from Arthur. She'd been working the morning shift for a while and he'd missed being able to eat dinner with her.

"Let me shake your hand, you've succeeded where we all failed," she said. "Midge is doing some good work in group now. How'd you manage it?"

Arthur's face felt hot. He didn't want to tell her. The diet part was too embarrassing.

"You're looking good, Arthur," Twila said. "Different. Something different about you. Your eyes look bigger. Bluer."

Arthur shrugged and glanced down at the chicken breast.

"I know what it is! You've lost weight," Twila said.

Arthur gazed longingly as Twila bit into her cheese steak. He watched with rapt attention as tiny specks of meat and cheese dropped down onto Twila's plate. The heady smell of steak and melted cheese and fried onions, the pile of golden French fries still sizzling with hot grease, made him weak. He glanced down at the salad and pale chicken breast on his tray and tried to calculate the calorie exchange if he succumbed to a steak sandwich. His eyes watered in self-pity.

He changed the subject. "Has she talked about seeing that kid ride into the sewer pipe?" he asked.

"She didn't see anything like that." Twila continued to chew as she answered. "Her little brother drowned in a ditch. She had nothing to do with it, but her parents blamed her."

"Wait a minute. She told me she watched a kid ride into a sewer pipe and drown."

"That's how she deals with her brother's death. She had sort of a breakdown when he died. Her parents split up after that. Then her father got married again."

"I've never seen a mother around here," Arthur said.

"I think she just ran off afterwards."

"But why blame Midge?"

"Her father was away at the time, apparently running around with the next Mrs. Ryder at that point. Midge's mother was off at some tennis match or something, and the babysitter was doing god-knows-what when the boy took off on his bike. Guess everyone felt guilty. Easiest to just blame Midge. You might say she was the sacrificial lamb."

Twila took the last bite of her cheese steak. "And you know the alien stone from hell? That was her brother's. That and the bear. MacDonald. She brought them with her, hardly ever let that stone out of her hands until you got her that dish garden."

Arthur pictured the stone nestled in the midst of the moss and violets. Like a coffin.

Twila had finished her meal. "Anyway, thanks for whatever you're doing."

"How come you're not married, Fats?" Midge asked him one afternoon, as they made their way along a corridor toward the therapy room.

"How do you know I'm not?" he said.

"Well, are you?"

"No," he admitted.

"Shacked up?"

He had to laugh.

"No."

"What, you some kind of freakin' queer?" she sneered.

"My girl walked out on me." He didn't usually speak about his personal life.

They walked on in silence until they reached the therapy room.

"Why'd she do that?" she said at the door.

"It's a long story," Arthur replied.

She studied his face. "No big deal. People fuckin' come, fuckin' go."

Midge made him weigh in at the nurses station every day, as soon as he arrived on his shift, and she kept a record of how many pounds he owed her. The days he didn't show a loss, Midge refused to talk in her group therapy and Arthur ran an extra mile before the next weigh in. After the initial fast drop, it got harder to shed on a daily basis. He tried to explain this to Midge.

"No excuses, Fat Boy," she said.

Twila cornered him in the employees lounge one evening as he stood contemplating a vending machine and fantasizing about a plate of fried chicken.

"Midge is making a real breakthrough in the group," Twila said. Her cologne smelled like apples. He leaned closer.

"You know, Art, I think she's been misdiagnosed." Twila had taken to calling him "Art." "I don't think she's borderline at all."

Arthur smiled. Another diagnosis dismantled.

"Oh, she's got serious problems," Twila went on. "That father of hers. And she adores him, God help her! I've seen how she looks at him. Good looking as hell. If I didn't know what a shit he was…then there's the under-aged stepmother. Not to mention her mother taking off like she did."

Arthur was conscious of how green Twila's eyes looked in the reflected light from the vending machine.

"The kid's had too many losses," Twila said. "There's nobody home for her. Unfortunately…."

Arthur sensed bad news coming.

"They'll be sending her home soon," Twila said.

"She won't want to go," he warned.

"She told the group that she has you under her thumb."

Arthur smiled. Now there was a real breakthrough, admitting to such a close relationship.

The window blind had been slashed…*where in god's name did she get scissors?*…and she had managed to flip her bed over onto its side. She had dragged the mattress down the hall into the shower and turned on the water, destroying the mattress. She had floated a dozen or so of her panatelas in the row of toilets, which was causing the other patients to gag.

He found her barricaded in the dining room, where she had upturned four tables to make a fortress. From behind her fort, she lobbed fruit and handfuls of something gooey, which Arthur discovered was strawberry pudding. He ducked an apple. A banana grazed his scalp. He maneuvered toward the fort, keeping low, like a commando, skidding on some pudding. He dove around the end table and before Midge could react, he pinned her arms to her side like a human straight jacket.

"Let me go, you freakin' dick brain!" she yelled. Legs flailing, she threw her head from side to side and tried to twist free.

Arthur held on. He saw Annabelle running through the door, Twila close on her heels, followed by two attendants, followed by Dr. Matthews, wearing his usual gray suit and tie and "well, well, what have we here?" demeanor.

"They're all coming," Arthur said into Midge's ear. "I know you're putting this on. Settle down or you'll be in restraints the rest of the summer. Is that what you want?"

She almost succeeded in biting his arm as Dr. Matthews and Annabelle rounded the fort. Midge kicked Annabelle in the knee, a move that sent the nurse to the floor. Dr. Matthews gestured for the two attendants to give Arthur a hand. One of them grabbed Midge's ankles and the other hoisted her around the waist, leaving Arthur still pinning her arms and avoiding her teeth.

He watched Dr. Matthews aim a syringe at Midge's arm, the needle about six inches from Arthur's face. Midge managed to flip a middle finger at Dr. Matthews before the sedative knocked her out.

Midge stayed in the restraining room for three days and nights until Dr. Matthews decided it was therapeutically safe to let her out. On the fourth day, Dr. Matthews called a family conference with Mr. Ryder, the new Mrs. Ryder, Midge of course, and Twila, since she was Midge's primary therapist and expected to have her under control.

"You should have heard it," Twila told Arthur later in the cafeteria. Arthur breathed in the aroma from Twila's big bowl of chicken potpie. He felt saliva gathering in his mouth.

"Dr. M. is saying he wants them all to get better acquainted, establish a bond, so that Midge feels more comfortable about coming home. 'Let's each examine our expectations.'" She mimicked Dr. Matthews' precise tight-lipped manner of well-enunciated syllables.

"Well, the 'expectation' theme never really got off the ground," Twila went on. "Midge called her stepmother a fat gold-digging sleaze who was pussy-whipping her father and then the stepmother practically flew out of her chair and smacked Midge across the face. Called her an insane little bitch who no one could be expected to live with and she certainly didn't intend to. Then Midge jumped up and dumped soda all over the sleaze...excuse me, the stepmother...and her sexy silk suit, which must have cost a small fortune, it was no J. C. Penney number, believe me." Twila paused to spoon potpie into her mouth. The act seemed erotic to Arthur. He lusted, his own baked fish and Caesar salad forgotten.

"Midge really did that?" he said.

"Oh, yeah. Turned the can upside down right in that woman's cleavage. You never heard such screeching, like a stuck pig. Dr. M turned pure white, just pure white, the color drained right out of his face."

"Then what?" He waited impatiently while Twila paused to take a drink of her iced tea.

"Then Ryder grabbed hold of his wife's arm...god, he's a good looking guy!...and dragged her out of the office while Midge and wife were still yelling at each other. He got her out into the hall and then he came back in and told Midge he'd deal with her later. Midge screamed at him that no way would she be coming home as long as the child-bride was there. So Mr. Ryder left, trying to straighten the front of his thousand dollar suede jacket the whole time, and Midge got sent back to her room to calm down."

Arthur heard the loud voices as soon as he rounded the corner of Midge's corridor. It had been four weeks since the family conference. Some days Midge cooperated, some days she refused to talk to anyone, even to Arthur. He wasn't sure if the girl was slipping into a depression or merely planning strategy.

The door to 60 East was half open and Arthur could see the two of them squaring off in the center of the room, Midge pulled up to her almost-five feet of height, hands clenched at her side. Her face was the color of a ripe tomato. She was yelling at her father, whose face was almost as red as Midge's.

"You fuckin' deserted me!" Midge was screaming. "And where've you been!"

"I never deserted you!" her father yelled back. "And watch your mouth."

"You did! You didn't care about any of us. You took off with fuckin' Lolita and you *abandoned* me," she wailed.

"We were all a mess after Timmy," her father said. "You weren't the only one, it wasn't all about *you*."

"You blamed me!" She shrieked and pounded his chest with her fists.

He grabbed her by the wrists and held on. Arthur stood inside the door and considered stepping between them, but decided to wait. He had no idea how Midge's father had gotten past the front guard and back here to Midge's room, but the scene looked cathartic. It could be the breakthrough of the century for Midge.

"You blamed it on me," Midge yelled again, trying to free her arms. "I would've gone in there after him. I loved him!"

"Midge, calm down, I know you loved him," Mr. Ryder said.

"I didn't even know he was gone!" Midge pulled against him trying to free her arms. Arthur thought of a small donkey digging in its hooves. "Where were you and *Mom?*"

Her father let go of her wrists. His shoulders slumped and he sat down on the edge of Midge's narrow bed. He picked up MacDonald and absently rubbed the top of the bear's head.

"Look, baby, I know it wasn't your fault." Mr. Ryder held a hand out toward her. "It was an awful accident. We couldn't see what was happening to *you* afterward."

"You went away."

Arthur could see Midge forcing herself to stay enraged, but her anger was slipping away. "You left *Mom*."

"Your mother left *me* a long time ago," he said wearily. "She just didn't move out 'til after Timmy."

Midge turned her back on her father and kicked her dresser hard, her plaid sneaker falling off when she did. She looked pathetic standing there with one shoe on, one shoe off, Arthur thought.

"Screw it," she snapped.

"Come here, baby," Mr. Ryder said. "I want you to come home."

"Not as long as that sleaze is in my house!"

"We'll work it out. Whatever it takes."

After another three weeks, Midge earned a reprieve for good behavior, and Arthur knew her remaining days at the hospital were limited. He had mixed feelings about her leaving. He had become used to the drama, it was part of his daily life these days.

"We're going on a trip, me, my dad and the whore mother," Midge informed Arthur one afternoon when he found her stuffing underwear and jeans into a duffel.

"Midge…." Arthur started.

"Yeah. Right. Be nice, get free. Let's go out in the yard. Want a cigar?"

"It's not yard time," Arthur said.

"Holy shit, Fats, don't you ever break a rule?"

They walked to the far end of the yard and Midge lit a panatela.

"How much did you lose?" she asked him through a mouthful of smoke.

"Enough. How sane did you get?"

"Enough," she grinned.

She looked around the yard. "What's with you and Twila? You screwin' her?"

"None of your damn business!" he exploded.

"Forget that other one, the one that ditched you. Grab onto Twila," she said.

"You think you know what's best for me?"

"Straight fuckin' A!"

He sat in Twila's small office the next day.

"They're going on a trip somewhere," he said.

"Yeah. The three of them together. That ought to be good."

"She promised she'd behave. Hard to imagine, though."

"The only way she got to go home."

"I'm gonna' miss her," Arthur said.

"She left this for you." Twila pushed a small bundle across the desk toward him. Arthur had an idea what it was, judging from the bulge. She had wrapped the stone in a piece of tablet paper and scribbled in nearly illegible handwriting:

"*See ya, Lard Ass. Keep it polished. Midge.*"

He was raking leaves and trimming plants in his garden when the mail came. The postmark read Ensenada, Mexico and the front of the postcard was a display of sandy beach. It was dated ten days after Midge left the hospital. "*We are here getting divorced,*" it read. "*Keep that stone shined, Cool Buns. Love, Midge.*"

Arthur flopped down on a lawn chair and laughed until he cried, startling a pair of gold finches at the thistle seed feeder. Mopping his eyes, he went into the kitchen, where Midge's stone lay on the window sill. He rubbed it against his shirt and held it up to the light, admiring the bits of color reflected on its pewter-like surface.

He could only imagine what she had put her father and step-mother through when she got home. Maybe nothing, maybe she'd been the penitent daughter, sweet and cooperative and…nah, he knew better. Whatever resources she'd used, she finally got her father back, thank you Dr. Freud.

What was it she'd advised him to do that last day they'd talked? Forget the one who ditched him and concentrate on Twila. Probably good advice. He kissed the stone soundly and replaced it on the window sill.

"Thanks, kid," he said.

SEISMIC SHIFT

Joanna's world began to change soon after her mother Estelle's seventieth birthday. She blamed the phone that she and her brothers had given their mother as a birthday gift.

The change was subtle on her mother's part...often not home in the afternoons when Joanna called her (whereas she had always been at home), telling Joanna she was "going out" but vague about where, and even more disturbing, her mother not always available to stay with Joanna's twin sons in the evenings when Joanna had a meeting at school, or wanted to go on a date, or out with girl-friends. Estelle had never passed up an opportunity to spend time with her grandsons, Michael and Joe, and it shocked Joanna when her mother began doing just that.

Joanna and her two older brothers had, after much discussion, agreed to buy a smart phone for their mother to replace the little flip phone she sometimes carried and sometimes forgot, and which didn't do much of anything except make phone calls. They presented Estelle with the phone as soon as dinner and the birthday cake had been consumed.

"What is this?" Estelle had said when she unwrapped the box and pulled out the sleek white piece. The family waited expectantly for Estelle to approve the gift.

"It's a smart phone, one of the latest models out there," Joanna's older brother Robert said.

"But I have a phone," Estelle protested.

"Your phone is a relic," Robert said. "We want you to be able to do more things with it. Have better protection when you're here alone. Or out somewhere. Suppose your car broke down!" He checked his own phone while he spoke and texted a reply with lightning speed.

Nearly fifty now, Robert ran the family business their father founded. He took life very seriously. Joanna couldn't recall seeing him dressed in anything other than his pin-striped suits, dark in the winter, gray in the summer, although she assumed, or rather *hoped*, he stripped down somewhat at home. He scolded Joanna regularly for dressing what he called "unprofessionally"…her skirts too short and her tops too tight. With her long dark hair, she probably did look unprofessional most of the time, but the students related to her look.

Joanna studied her mother's face as Estelle studied the new phone. Not good. Estelle did not look as pleased as they had hoped for. In fact she looked annoyed.

"The phone I have is perfectly fine," Estelle said, laying the gift carefully back in its box. "Thank you all very much. It was sweet of you, but these newer phones are much too complicated."

Joanna's brother Carl pulled out his own phone, ran his finger across the screen and held it up to their mother. Joanna caught a glimpse of two little blonde girls smiling into the camera, the same two little girls who now stood close to their mother.

"Look, you can put pictures of your grandkids on it, show your friends," he said.

Of her two brothers, Carl was Joanna's favorite. He was sunny and gentle and capable of thinking beyond his own ego, unlike Robert and her, she always thought. The only one of them who could hug people without anxiety. She smiled at him with affection, taking in the jeans and sweater that made him look like a college kid instead of a low-paid but highly visible forty-plus year old sportscaster for cable television and father of two little daughters.

"Well, I don't know," Joanna's mother said. "I like to look at pictures in an album rather than on a phone." Her mother always dealt in people, feelings, and clothes. Not technology. She had wrapped her pale blue Donna Karan sweater across her chest like a fashionable vest of armor and continued to stare at the new phone, which looked abandoned now in its fancy gift box.

"I can show you how to use it, Grandma," Joanna's son Michael said.

"Me, too," his twin brother Joe chimed in. "It's easy, Grandma. We'll show you!" Twelve now, the twins were experts with modern electronics, like most boys their age.

Estelle had pulled the boys to her, one in the crook of each arm, and hugged them hard. "I'll have to see," she had said. Which meant "don't push me." They all knew when not to push. Estelle might seem malleable but she did things in her own time.

Joanna was surprised the next day when, on the way home from the middle school where she was assistant principal, she called her mother and there was no answer. Except for her volunteer Wednesdays at the hospital, Estelle was usually home in the afternoon. She had been a stay-at-home mom all the time Joanna was growing up, and Joanna still liked the thought of her mother being always available.

Remembering something about Robert and Marsha having a dinner party that evening, she called to inquire if Estelle might be there.

"Mom doesn't answer the phone, is she over there?" she asked when her sister-in-law answered.

"No, she called, she's coming at five-forty-five," Marsha replied, brisk and organized like Robert. Joanna could hear her nephew, Robert Jr., making some kind of racket in the background, continuing an argument with his mother in tones only fifteen-year olds can muster.

"Oh well, " Joanna said. Her mother was all right then. But where the heck was she?

As the youngest of three children, and a daughter arriving after two sons, Joanna had always felt special in her family. Her brothers watched over her on the playground, and later at school, and her father called her his little princess. None of them had approved of her marrying Jason, but she had fallen head over heels for him and when she persisted in the romance, they had finally given her a spectacular wedding, plus a honeymoon in the Caribbean. The twins were the only good thing that had come from the marriage, which had lasted exactly four years. Joanna had divorced Jason after too many young blonde diversions on his part and a fondness for the white powder.

Her mother had held her together all during the heartbreaking months before and after the divorce and even now, years later, she couldn't imagine what she would do without her mother's shoulder to lean on. When her father died eight years ago, she knew it was her turn to help her mother and she had kept her as busy as she could, mainly by involving her even more with the twins.

"Where were you yesterday?" Joanna settled on a stool in her mother's kitchen the next day, and spotted a Domino's pizza box on the counter by the sink. She pointed at the box. "What's this?" Her mother was not of the pizza generation. She always considered it extravagant and a little slothful to order in pizza.

"I ordered it with my new phone, on the way home from the mall." Her voice and her face exuded pride. "The delivery boy arrived the same time that I did. So convenient."

She appeared more animated than Joanna had seen her these past eight years. She's glowing, Joanna thought.

"You've learned how to use your new phone? You're going to keep it?"

"Yes, " she said. "And I have apps." She picked up the pizza box and slid it into the refrigerator. "Oh, would you like a piece?" she asked, an afterthought.

Joanna shook her head.

"There's all sorts of things I can do with it," she said. "With the apps, like the GSP."

"GPS," Joanna corrected. "Did Carl show you all this stuff?"

"No, a friend showed me," she said, smiling. Her smile seemed secretive to Joanna. She wanted to know more but she needed to get home.

"About the twins, can you stay with them this evening? I have a meeting at school and it's really important that I be there." She assumed her mother would be more than willing. She was always so proud of Joanna's position at the school and helped her all she could.

"Oh, I can't, Dear, I'm sorry." She looked genuinely sorry. "I've made some plans."

She poured a glass of spring water and offered some to Joanna, who could only shake her head stupidly at this unexpected response.

"Where are you going?" she finally asked.

"Oh, out," Estelle said.

"Robert, who is Mother going out with tonight?" Joanna demanded as soon as she pulled away from her mother's house.

"Don't know. Why?" Robert's voice sounded muffled. She pictured him cradling a phone between a pin-striped shoulder and his cheek while he continued marking important papers that would be piled on his desk, formerly her father's desk.

"She's going out and she won't tell me where."

"I'll look into it," Robert said, his attention elsewhere.

Joanna punched Carl's number into her phone. No answer.

She didn't talk to her mother for several days, between activities that kept her tied up at school and Estelle not being home the times she called. When they did talk, Estelle was filled with excitement.

"Oh, Joanna, you'll never believe it! I'm on line now," she said.

"You don't even have a computer!"

"Oh, yes, I have a beautiful new computer," she said.

Joanna didn't know what to say.

"Joanna? Are you still there, dear?"

"I'm here. When did you get a computer, Mother? You hate that stuff." She was used to her mother being incompetent about technological things.

"Not any more, now that I understand it," Estelle said. "I've found all sorts of things on the internet."

"Mother, how did you even know what kind of a computer to get?" Joanna heard the exasperation in her own voice. Her mother seemed like someone she didn't know right now.

"Oh, a friend helped me," Estelle said.

"I want to see it." She was determined to dig through this electronic haze and find her mother again.

"I'm about to go out," Estelle said. "Can you wait and come over tomorrow, Dear?" And her mother hung up, leaving Joanna feeling more exasperated than ever.

"Robert, is Mother seeing someone?" Her ear burned from the phone jammed against it.

"You mean like a psychiatrist?" he said, distracted no doubt by some business task.

"Like a MAN."

Robert paused for what seemed a long time. "What do you mean?" he finally asked. She had his attention now.

"I mean," she spoke slowly, as if to one of her students, "that she is always busy…out…ever since we got her that phone. And she glows."

"She what?"

"Glows. She glows. I think she's got a boyfriend."

"Impossible," Robert said.

After work the next afternoon Joanna drove directly to her mother's house. Regardless of Robert scoffing at the idea, she knew better. She had a sixth sense about it and she needed to find out what was going on with her mother. She hoped against hope that Estelle wasn't involved with some man who might be after her money. Her mother was a wealthy and vulnerable widow, easy prey for a slick man. Jason had taught her how treacherous some guys could be.

A white J. T. Computers, Inc. van was parked in the driveway of her mother's house.

She tapped on the front door and stepped into the familiar living room. As always, she looked around admiringly at the beautiful paintings and sculptures her parents had brought back from their trips abroad. She had grown up with artwork from all over the world, as well as the beautifully carved tables and credenza that graced the living room. She touched the back of her favorite upholstered chair as she passed through the room, a big comfortable chair where she had spent many hours reading over the years. She called "haloo" and followed the murmur of voices into what used to be her father's den.

Their heads came together, their shoulders almost touching, both staring intently at the monitor, her mother and this---man. Joanna felt the floor move under her feet like a seismic shift.

"Come in, Joanna! We're in a chat room." They continued to watch the screen for a few minutes before finally turning toward her.

"Hi. Jack Tandler." The man stood and reached out to shake Joanna's hand. He was tall, like her father had been. But there the resemblance stopped. Her father had been ruggedly handsome, trim, with dark hair (dyed eventually) and wonderful brown eyes. He had been a vain man, like Robert, and her. She thought of her favorite picture of him in their family album, wearing a black tux, his arms around her and Jason at their wedding. It's how she always remembered him.

Jack Tandler, on the other hand, was a little overweight, even for his height, and he had blue eyes and curly reddish hair that was turning gray and dissolving into the temples. He wore a red plaid flannel shirt. He also possessed a grin that made you grin back.

"Are you from the computer company?" She hoped that would explain his presence, although down deep she knew better.

"Right," he said. "I'm the computer guy. And the phone man."

Joanna's mother started laughing. She hadn't heard her laugh like that for a long time. She sounded young.

"Jack showed me how to use my new phone," she said. "At the CellularTech store at the Mall."

Her mother and a store clerk? Estelle laughed again. Joanna could tell from her mother's expression that she knew what her daughter was thinking.

"Your mother and I got talking about her new phone and that led to computers and she decided she wanted one. I helped her buy one and set it up," he explained.

"Robert, Mother has a boyfriend," she blurted into her phone as soon as she left her mother's house.

"A what?" Robert muttered, distracted as usual.

"A boyfriend. He's there now."

"Hmm." She heard papers rustling in the background.

"Listen to me." She tried to sound calm. "Mother bought a computer. She's on the Internet. She and this man, this *boyfriend*, are at the house on the new computer. They're in a chat room!"

Robert remained silent a long while. "Who's the boyfriend?" he finally asked.

"He owns a computer business," Joanna said. "He showed Mother how to use that damn phone we gave her. Then he helped her buy a computer. They're like a couple of lovebirds in front of that screen." She heard her voice escalating. Her mother was too old to have a boyfriend.

"I'll look into it." Robert hung up on her.

She called Carl. He, at least, would take this seriously, do something about it.

"Who, Jack? He's a nice guy," Carl said.

"You *know* him?"

"I know the whole family, so do you," he said. "Went to school with Stu, his son. Stu has CellularTech at the Mall, it's where I picked up Mom's phone."

She couldn't speak, her thoughts whirling.

"That's why I told Mom to go over there for instructions on the phone. I told her to talk to Jack. He's there a lot, helps Stu out."

She smacked the steering wheel of her van so hard her eyes watered. "You set her up! Your own mother!"

Carl laughed. "Take it easy, Sis. Talk to you later."

Joanna was busy at school with the pre-holiday schedule, but at her mother's request, she asked Jack Tandler to teach a computer workshop for the sixth grade. She suspected her mother had an ulterior motive. Jack was good with the kids, which surprised her. He had been widowed twenty years ago, and she knew he had a grown son. But she just hadn't thought of him relating to kids. She'd wanted him to be a jerk so she could dislike him.

After the class, they ate lunch together in the school cafeteria.

"I love your mother very much. I want to marry her," he said over plates of starchy macaroni and cheese.

Joanna busied herself stirring sugar into her coffee. He didn't press her for a response, just talked about how savvy her students seemed to be with computers. When he left, Joanna felt more mixed up than ever, because she was beginning to like the man.

Later that same day she relayed their conversation to her mother.

"I want to marry Jack, too," her mother said. They stood in Estelle's kitchen, Joanna near tears, her mother looking serene.

"I don't want things to change," Joanna said. "I'm worried about how Dad would feel."

"Eight years. That's a long time to hang onto the past. Your dad would be all right with this."

Maybe he would, Joanna thought, but it scared her to death. She wanted things to stay just like they were.

"Not yet," she pleaded. "Please, not yet. It's too soon."

Her mother hesitated. "Maybe you're right. Maybe it is too soon. I'll have to think about it some more." Her expression had gone from happy to sad just like that and Joanna felt like a villain. But she could not bear the thought of things changing so drastically.

Carl sounded angry when Joanna answered her phone the next day. A Saturday, she was doing the usual swish cleaning of the house, having sent the boys off to the movies.

"Mother has decided not to marry Jack," he said. "What in God's name did you say to her? What have you done?"

"Nothing," she said, caught off guard. She didn't know *what* she had done. She pushed away a niggling little reminder of her conversation with Estelle the day before.

"You told her you weren't ready for her to get married again. Mom has a right to a happy life that doesn't revolve around you and all your needs. You're a selfish brat!" he said and hung up.

Carl had never spoken to her like that in all her life. Selfish? No. She wasn't. She was thinking of *her mother*. Her father. Of the family. Maybe herself, too, but just a little.

Robert sounded cold when she called him. "When are you going to grow up? " he said. "Mom gave up her plans to marry Jack because you begged her not to. What's the matter with you, anyway!" he snapped and hung up on her.

She stood under a hot shower and cried. It didn't help. She walked naked into her kitchen and poured herself a glass of wine, hoping the boys wouldn't walk in on her. It helped, but not enough. She went back into her bedroom and stood looking at herself in the mirror over the dresser. She looked like shit. Puffy red eyes, wet hair hanging in stringy black ropes, and lately too much extra weight.

"When are you going to grow up?" Robert had said. *Wasn't she already grown up?* She was doing a good job of handling a career and twin sons and a house. She thought she was giving her mother a purpose to her life, helping her and the boys.

Carl had called her a selfish brat. Said Mom had a right to her own life, without taking care of her...*her only daughter!*...all the time. Something like that. It was the shock of it, that her mother could want a different life, and that her brothers could think such awful things about her. Of course she wanted her mother to be happy. How could they think differently? They didn't understand.

She called Carl back later that day, confused and feeling contrite, although she wasn't sure why.

"They're a great pair," he said. "Jack makes her happy. Isn't that what you want for her?"

She had a lump in her throat and couldn't answer right away.

"Sis?" Carl said gently. "We're all going to be okay. She's not going anywhere."

"Promise?"

"Promise."

"I do want her to be happy. I'm just afraid."

She paced the room, counting off twelve lengths back and forth each time, while she thought about her mother being married to someone other than her father. She replayed the hours her mother had spent consoling her when she divorced Jason. And the devotion her mother had always shown to all her children and grandchildren. She had to admit her mother seemed so much happier these days, which triggered guilt feelings in Joanna. It made her feel selfish, as though she was trying to deny her mother this happiness. Finally she called her mother.

"The boys said it's my fault you called off your wedding," Joanna said. "I feel awful. But I can't help it, I'm so scared to lose you. Everything will change if you marry Jack. Everything has already changed a lot."

"You aren't going to lose me, Joanna," her mother said.

"I thought you were happy helping me take care of the twins. I thought that was what you wanted." Joanna burst into fresh tears. "And I'm so afraid of how Daddy will feel if you get married. I know, I know, it's silly maybe, he's gone, but I can't help..."

"Joanna, dear, listen to me. I want you to listen very carefully. Before your father died, right before he slipped into the coma, he said he wanted me to get married again if I ever found someone who made me happy. He made me promise that I would do that. Your father and I had a wonderful marriage, and for a few years I never thought I'd want to remarry. There was no man who could hold a candle to your father." Her voice caught and she paused.

"Mom..." Joanna started, talking through a sob, but her mother stopped her.

"But the last few years I've been lonely," Estelle went on, her voice normal again. "I love you, and your brothers, and all your children, and you have made me happy, you gave me a reason to live after your father died. But lately I've wanted to have someone of my own again. I'm ready for marriage again because your father and I had such a good marriage. That's the way it works. I'm not afraid to love again."

Joanna was crying harder. "I never knew Daddy made you promise that."

"He wanted me to be happy after he was gone," Estelle said. Joanna could tell her mother was crying now, too.

"I never knew you were lonesome either," Joanna said when her voice came under control. "I thought we were keeping you busy enough so you wouldn't be."

"And you did. But it's time for you to stop trying to take care of me and spend more time with your own friends, go out on some dates, don't let all the disappointment over your marriage keep you from doing that. And do more fun things with your boys."

Do more with my boys! "Do you think I don't do enough for the twins?" Joanna felt fear of a different kind than before, a fear that she was failing as a mother in Estelle's eyes.

"You take very good care of your sons," Estelle assured her. "But you don't have enough fun with them, maybe because you have so much responsibility in your job. Can you think of the last time you and the boys went somewhere together, on a vacation?"

Nothing came to mind and she felt even more of a failure.

"Well, why don't you try to think of something you can all do together? You don't have to keep making sure I'm all right. I'm fine. I really am. And I'm happy. I want you to be happy, too. I want us both to be happy."

Her mother's words brought on fresh tears. She eventually wiped at her eyes and blew her nose hard and took a deep breath. She had to at least *try* to accept what was happening. What other choice did she have?

"Could the twins and I come on your honeymoon with you?" Joanna asked, trying to make a joke even though she felt her world shifting and knew her words had okayed the shift.

Her mother laughed that same young laugh Joanna heard the time she saw her beside Jack at the computer. "Does that mean you're giving me permission to get married?" she asked.

"I guess so." It came out like a whisper. She cleared her throat and tried again. "Yes."

Estelle and Jack married that June, a small elegant wedding held at the United Methodist Church where Joanna had grown up. She was her mother's matron of honor. Robert and Carl walked their mother down the aisle and officially turned her over to Jack. Joanna thought her mother was the most beautiful bride she'd ever seen, radiant in a silky blue gown, holding a dozen yellow roses in her arms. Her mother held her close and whispered "I love you" in Joanna's ear before she and Jack climbed into a car decorated with paper flowers and streamers and left on their honeymoon.

On her way home from work the following Monday, Joanna called her older brother at his office. "Have you heard from them yet?"

"It's only been two days since they left." As usual, Robert sounded annoyed at being interrupted.

"Will you let me know?"

"Umm," Robert said.

She disconnected and called Carl at work.

"I can't get used to it, another man in her life," she said.

"She's happy," Carl said. "Jack pulled her into the Twenty-first Century. They're great together, Sis. Be happy for them."

"Will things ever be the same again?'

"They never were," Carl said.

She didn't know what he meant but it sounded profound. She'd have to think about it.

That evening, after the twins went to bed, Joanna sat on the edge of her own bed with a photo album her mother had made for her when she and Jason were married. There she was at two years old, with her mother holding her on the swing in their backyard. Her sixth birthday party, Estelle setting a cake with six candles in front of her. *Oh my God, graduation!* She looked geeky. Big horn rimmed glasses, that awful haircut. And Dad with his arm across her shoulders, looking proud.

She looked better in her wedding pictures, with Jason on one side of her and her parents on the other. And then that picture of her in the hospital holding the twins---she looked like the wrath of God. But there was her mother bending over her, always right there at her side, all her life.

It won't ever be the same, no matter what Carl says.

The ring of the phone startled her. Mother and Jack.

"We miss you," they said. Joanna gasped and laughed and said she missed them, too.

"We'll call and let you know where we are while we travel," Jack said.

"Don't forget." Joanna swallowed and held back tears.

She had a million questions for them, but the connection was not good and they soon ended the call. She tried Carl's number even though it was late. She heard TV noise in the background.

"Mother and Jack just called," she said.

"You okay?" he asked.

She thought about that. How could she be okay? *I'm never going to have my mother back, not the way we were.*

She glanced down at the photo album on her lap. All these family memories that her mother had made for her. She had never made an album of the twins and her, their family activities, even when Jason was around. She had pictures stuffed in drawers, but she'd always been too busy at work to do anything with them, or busy getting divorced, or preoccupied watching over her mother.

She realized she was still holding the phone to her ear with Carl on the other end, waiting while she sorted things out in her mind.

"Yeah, I'm okay," she said, only half-sure. Her thoughts took her to Ocean City, a trip with the twins this summer. They'd rent a small apartment, spend all day on the beach, eat in a touristy restaurant along the Boardwalk. Take pictures of each other and "selfies" of the three of them huddled under a big beach umbrella.

"Yeah, I'm okay," she repeated. *At least I will be.*

She stared at her phone, lost in a myriad of thoughts about beaches, and photo albums, and her mother and Jack off somewhere on a honeymoon. On impulse she googled Ocean City rental apartments on the phone and perused pictures of attractive houses and apartment buildings. One in particular caught her eye. A white frame building set back from the sidewalk, with steps leading up to a front porch that was shaded by striped awning. A block from the beach. *Nice.* Pricey. But she could swing it if she packed picnic lunches and they ate breakfast in. She clicked on the picture and looked at shots of the interior--- two bedrooms, kitchen, living room. She liked what she saw. School was out for the summer. She saw no reason why they couldn't leave soon. Her excitement grew at the thought of a week at the shore with Joe and Mike. She dug her credit card out of her purse, turned back to her phone, and began to book the vacation.

Author's Note

I'm sometimes asked where my stories come from. "Are the characters really some part of you?" My stories usually reflect something going on in my life at the time. For instance, *The Four Poster*, which won an honorable mention in a Central PA Magazine writing contest, was written at a time when a number of older relatives were entering nursing homes. I wanted to explore the emotions a person might have during this major change in his or her life. I wrote *Drumbeat Heartbeat* when Gere and I traveled through the west. I fell in love with Taos, N.M. and the Pueblo Indians we met there. The story, which won third place in another Central PA Magazine contest, was an attempt to capture the life of one young Indian man as he juggled tradition and contemporary times.

Tossed Out started as a tongue-in-cheek piece after I had thrown a lot of aging food out of our refrigerator. I was a therapist for ten years, so this story took a path through phobias and other psychological problems. *Breakthrough*, one of my favorite stories, also reflects some of my former career. I have Duncan Alderson to thank for setting me off on this story; we "students" at Rabbit Hill Writers Studio were instructed to write a story based on key words we pulled from a vase. The only word I remember now is "shoelace." The story developed from that. My apologies to those who are sensitive to rough language in this and any of the other stories. Just trying to "stay true to my characters."

The Contest Winner was an impulse story that showed up in my imagination one evening while I watched Gere work his daily crossword puzzle. I'd wanted to write about the inner world of a shy isolated woman who longed to feel important, the kind of person I call "a poor soul," not noticed by the rest of the world. Such a woman and crossword puzzles came together for me in this story.

Seismic Shift (my editor Ann Stewart came up with this lively title) was one of the first stories I wrote at Rabbit Hill. Originally titled *Cell Phone*, it was another impulse story that came to me one evening when I was trying to figure out the apps and buttons on my cell phone. I thought it would be fun to explore what happens to the relationship between a mother and daughter when the mother becomes "high tech."

Down for the Count---I have no idea how this story got into my imagination other than the fact that I liked the character's name and wanted to write a story about him. Conrad Shaltzhammer was another "lost soul." I brought psychology into this story, too, and gave Conrad an obsessive-compulsive problem, in order to lead him into the trouble that led him to his future.

My favorite story has always been *Old Blue*, which first appeared in Ann Stewart's literary journal PHASE. That's Old Blue on the book cover, just as I see him in the story (thank you, Cindy Zollman, for this photo!). I wanted to write about great blue herons, which fascinate me, and the feel of being on the Chesapeake Bay and its nearby rivers, where Gere and I and the kids spent most of our summers. I used this setting to explore the complicated feelings between parents and children following a family tragedy.

I hope readers enjoy these stories as much as I enjoyed writing them. All the proceeds from the sale of this book will go to the wonderful charity, Doctors without Borders, which does so much good for people in poor countries of the world.

Peggy Frailey
June 29, 2017

Made in the USA
Middletown, DE
06 December 2017